HEATHER McCORKLE

CLAWED
& CORNERED

CHILDREN OF FENRIR NOVELLA

CITY OWL
PRESS

This book is a work of fiction. Names, characters, places, and incidents either are products of the author's imagination or are used fictitiously. Any resemblance to actual events or locales or persons, living or dead, is entirely coincidental and not intended by the author.

CLAWED & CORNERED
Children of Fenrir, Novella

CITY OWL PRESS
www.cityowlpress.com

Cover Design by Mibl Art. All stock photos licensed appropriately.

Edited by Yelena Casale.

For information on subsidiary rights, please contact the publisher at info@cityowlpress.com.

Print Edition ISBN: 978-1-64898-032-9

Digital Edition ISBN: 978-1-64898-031-2

Printed in the United States of America

For all the great loves that almost were.

PRAISE FOR HEATHER McCORKLE

"Kickass women, Icelandic warriors, and plenty of action!"
— Kait Ballinger, Bestselling Author of The Execution Underground Series

"The characters have lots of depth to them and are strong, sexy and fun. A fabulous story line full of magic and danger that I was pulled into from the first page. I can't wait to read more of this series. I loved it."
— Petula Winmill, Book Reviewer

"Holy werewolves, Batman! What did I just read!! A winning combination of romance and heat, action, and drama, not to mention plenty of Norse lore and mythology to make a paranormal lover combust! This story was unique and quite different from the shifter stories we've come to know and love. Ms. McCorkle did a marvelous job with weaving her story and I am so looking forward to what's coming next."
— Katrina Berry, Book Reviewer

"Excellent book!! Not your average shifter book. I really like the Norse bent to the storyline. Couldn't put it down and anxiously awaiting book 2 of the series."
— Susan Hall, Book Reviewer

"What a great story this is! One of the best things about it is that I can't think of a book to compare it too. The reason why I love that, is because the story is just so unique. Which is why I kept turning the page! Loved it!"
— Ali Cross, USA Today Bestselling Author of Young Adult Fantasy

"There's trouble in the Dragon Empire, the kind that could start a war between dragons and the races of people...For those who love fantasy, dragons and a sweet love story, this book is definitely a must read for you!"
— Geeky Book Gal

CHILDREN OF FENRIR

RECOMMENDED READING ORDER

CHAPTER ONE

SONYA

I have a monumental taste for bad men. No, I don't mean I have monumentally bad taste in men, though that's true as well. No matter how one looks at it, that's why I was drawn to Raul's fine leather-clad body when he walked through the door of my bar. Tall, dark, and dangerous looking, he was everything I desired and nothing I needed. His eyes locked onto mine and held them like an industrial strength magnet. As he wove his way through the tables of people, I tensed, preparing a moment too late to call out when he stepped in the path of a couple of guys playing darts. Not that he would have heard me over the Friday night din of bad country music and drunks.

The idiots either didn't see him or didn't care because the portly one drew his dart back and let it fly. TD&D snatched it right out of the air like something from a movie, his gaze shooting toward the players. One moment he held the dart in his hand, the next his arm was down by his side. I didn't even realize what he had done until I heard the sharp metal 'thunk' resonate into wood. The sound drew my gaze to the bright red and blue plastic feathers thrust up between two of the player's fingers where his hand rested on the bar. The man snatched his hand against his side and took a step back.

"Damn, man, watch what the fuck you're doing!" The second player said.

TD&D grinned, exposing perfect white teeth with canines that were just a little longer than normal. "I was," he said in a voice that rumbled as if bordering on the edge of a growl.

Absently mopping up the remnants of glass rings on the bar top, I watched as TD&D sauntered in my direction. Not all men can pull off a saunter. This guy not only did it with class, but he also made it look smoking hot. The tight black designer jeans accentuating the promising bulge of his crotch didn't hurt matters, nor did the black nylon motorcycle jacket. I caught a flash of some sort of patch on the back of his jacket, but couldn't tell what it was from my angle. Before he could catch me staring at his goods and get the wrong impression, I forced my eyes upward. The black shirt hugging his fit body shone like silk, the gold buttons matching the brilliant flecks in his brown eyes. Designer cowboy boots that cost more than a day's pay with tips peeked out from his jeans. I shook my head and turned my attention back to cleaning.

Sure, it had been over a year since I'd gotten laid, but most good looking guys didn't affect me this strongly. Out of my peripheral vision, I saw that I wouldn't be able to avoid him much longer. He was walking straight up to the bar, and the only empty stool was right in front of me. The moment I decided to find something else to do anywhere but there, I looked up and he was suddenly settling onto the stool. How the hell he had moved that fast through a crowded bar, I had no idea. Unless of course I was stalling subconsciously. Otherworldly brown eyes with gold shooting out from the pupil like rays of an eclipsed sun snagged a hold of mine. I tried to look away but those brilliant eyes would not let me. Something haunted hid in them.

"Hello," he said through a disarming smile, those eyes never leaving mine.

The lack of pickup line or wandering gaze left me at a loss for words. It took me several moments just to muster up a "Hello," in return.

"I would love a glass of your top shelf Syrah, please," he said.

One of my brows lifted of its own accord. Wine snob; didn't see that coming. Figured. "Coming right up."

It took a lot to surprise me as a bartender, and it threw me completely off my game. On my way to the wine fridge at the end of the bar, I regained as much of my cool professional mask as I could. I grabbed our best Syrah from the fridge's red wine section, popped the cork, and poured a generous glass before returning the bottle. The entire time I felt TD&D's gaze on me and I didn't mind one bit. Though he oozed danger, something about him also felt very refined and proper. It was a strange and intriguing combination.

"Kinda busy for a weeknight," he commented over the din of conversation and music pouring from the bar's sound system. He had a nice voice, just deep enough to vibrate along one's skin, but smooth like he'd never smoked.

I nodded. "This place is always hopping."

He gave me a cover guy smile as his eyes flicked across me. "It's clear why."

Not exactly a cheap pick up line, but it was close, too close. I cast my gaze skyward and started to make my way down the bar.

The deep, little laugh that came from him managed to sound confident and contrite at the same time. "I meant it as an observation and compliment, not the cheap pick up line it sounded like."

I cast a half-smile his way. "It was creepishly cliche," I agreed.

He returned my smile and the air in the room suddenly seemed clearer, more inviting. It wasn't the perfect teeth with canines just a touch too long, or the rakishly handsome appearance they gave him. The effect came from a deep charisma very few people possessed, the kind of thing that made you want to be around someone without being able to put a finger on why.

"You hungry, Top Shelf?" I asked. I cringed inwardly and prepared myself for the pickup line that set me up for. What had I been thinking, phrasing it like that? But then, I hadn't, that was the thing. This guy threw me off my game in a big way.

As his gaze moved over my low-cut shirt and back up, his lips pulled into a smirk. "Yes, thank you. I would love a burger—as rare as your cook is allowed to leave it, and fries."

Since his eyes had taken a brief trip up my body, I allowed mine to do the same to him. "Cheat day for you?" Clearly he hit the gym, a lot, and that usually meant health nut as well. Guys like that tended to be a bit too judgmental about how a woman looked for my taste. I polished a glass while I waited for his answer, hoping I was wrong.

He shrugged one shoulder. "No need for cheat days with a balanced diet." The answer rang too close to health nut for my liking.

I tilted my head toward the opening between the bar and the overhead liquor cabinet and hollered the order back to Joe in the kitchen.

"Coming right up, gorgeous," he called back.

TD&D's eyes narrowed into a fierce look that made things low in my body tingle. "You should report his disrespectful ass to the owner," he said through a literal growl.

A laugh burst from me. "Wouldn't do any good. That bastard's even worse."

His muscles tensed like he was ready to rise from his stool. "Sounds like someone needs to be taught how to treat a lady."

I held a hand up. "Whoa, put your cape away. I don't need anyone to rescue me."

He sat down fast. "Oh no, I...uh...sorry, I didn't mean it that way."

I cocked my head at him and raised a brow, but refrained from responding. They never "meant it that way".

His face scrunched up into an adorable, beseeching look that had probably gotten him out of every disciplinary situation from birth to college. That magnetic golden gaze—the kind that leaves you a bit speechless because of the beauty behind it—tried to suck me in again. It was all the more powerful because he knew its effect, and I could see that in the depths of it.

"I'm sorry, really. I have a feeling you can take care of yourself and then some, and I like that," he said in a voice that slid over me smooth as silk, raising goosebumps. "Let me backtrack out of the worst start ever, with the most interesting person I've met ever, please." He paused and let his smile work its magic on me. I couldn't help it; I smiled back like a fool. I mean, Hel, he had said interesting, not beautiful. It impressed me. He went on. "I'm here on a bit of a walk-about. What do I absolutely need to visit in the area before going home?"

I decided to see if he was just a gym rat, or if he actually put those muscles to good use. My mind tried to take that to dirty places, and succeeded. I leaned over the bar, getting close enough he'd be able to hear me over the increasing clamor of chatter. And hey, it got me a good whiff of his leather and pine scent, not that overpowering cologne, but authentic trees and outdoors. I played it cool with a coy smile. "Depends on whether or not you're willing to get your designer boots dirty. If so, the Lupine Trail along Misery Ridge has a view that is well worth the hike."

The grin that split his tempting lips lit his eyes with a genuinely pleased shine that warmed my stomach and sent tingling fingers tracing down to make my vulva muscles tighten. "I would love to check that out."

Though I was bending over, offering a nice view down the v of my AC/DC t-shirt, his gaze never left mine. So the guy was more than pretty eyes, a Hollywood face, and designer clothes. Nice, really nice.

His mouth opened, but a pushy customer interrupted him by hollering for me from down the bar. Smile turning apologetic, I whisked off the serve the needy. The place really was hopping for a weeknight. Every table was full and only two bar seats were left empty, both next to TD&D. They'd been occupied when he arrived, but the little stunt with the dart had apparently made the patrons want to be elsewhere. All except for the two I saw approaching out of my peripheral. The oversized black cowboy hat stuck out like a sore thumb, a thumb I dreaded seeing each night.

Looking up slow and dramatic like, Stetson—as I'd come to think of him because of that ridiculous hat—met my gaze and winked one muddy brown eye at me. He swaggered his way to the bar in a gait that suggested his pants bordered on the painful side of being a bit too tight. The heels of working cowboy boots clicked an uneven rhythm that revealed his old bull riding injuries. I sneered at him in response to his coy look. Undeterred, he grinned and licked his lips, revealing a missing tooth behind his canines. The guy with him glared TD&D down as he strutted up to the empty stool on the right side of him. Damn, he was the one who'd thrown the dart. Things were about to get interesting.

"Sonya, this guy bothering you?" Stetson asked.

I rolled my eyes. "Duane, even if I were a tender princess, this guy wouldn't bother me half as much as you do."

Duane Stetson—my made-up surname for him, probably not his real one—rested both elbows on the bar and leaned as close as he could get to me. I took a step back to grab a bottle of Jack for a patron and put a bit more distance between Duane and myself.

"Well, hot and bothered wasn't what I meant," Duane drawled, thickening his Idaho accent for effect as he licked his lips.

Ugh. I didn't even try to fight the grossed-out look that came over me. Ignoring it, Duane went on. "Why don't you let me take you out to dinner after you get off?"

Slinging together a Jack and Coke without taking my narrowed glare off him, I answered, "I've decided to swear off food."

Nodding like the idiot he was, Duane's smile grew. "I respect a woman who knows when to diet, but girl, you are smoking. You don't need to shed any pounds."

I gave him a tight-lipped smile. "And I respect a guy who doesn't judge women by their bodies," I said in a carefully controlled voice.

Confusion clouded his eyes, which kind of made them the color of excrement. Or maybe that was just the cynicism he was raising in me. "Ah, come on. I meant it as a compliment. No need to go all feminist on me, Miss Ph.D." With that, he turned his back on me and plopped onto the stool to TD&D's left.

Both Duane and his friend leaned onto the bar and faced TD&D, all smiles and slimeball. The pissed look on TD&D's face made me think he was going to jump to my defense like a knight in shining armor, but he didn't. I wasn't sure if I was disappointed or flattered that he had paid attention to the fact that I liked to handle my own crap. He turned a look on Duane's friend that could make a lesser man pee his pants. Duane's friend swallowed hard but maintained his cocky look.

Sensing the brewing brawl, I tried to keep them in my peripheral as I slung a few drinks to people down the bar. When I turned my back I overheard Duane say, "Damn, that is one fine ass."

My teeth clenched. A glass slammed hard enough onto the wooden bar to ensure I'd have to check it for cracks. "Drop the disrespectful comments, now," TD&D's voice rumbled.

"Or what?" Duane egged him on. When TD&D didn't respond, Duane went on. "You'll shut it for me, pretty boy? Sonya can take care of herself."

"Oh, I don't doubt that, but I don't like people who are disrespectful to women. And now that you know that, if you keep running your mouth, you'll be offending me," TD&D said in that sexy, scary voice that promised bad things.

In hopes of heading off a fight, I strode down to them, hands on my hips. TD&D fixed Duane with a smile that made the cowboy look like he was staring at a trig question. "How about we handle this like grownups in a way that doesn't get any of us thrown out. You boys up for a game of darts?" TD&D asked.

Duane's friend leaped from his stool, a big, goofy smile splitting his face. "Hell yeah we are!"

Inwardly, I cringed. Duane liked to hustle guys at darts on a regular basis. He was pretty good at it. He slapped TD&D on the shoulder hard enough it would have staggered most men, but TD&D didn't budge an inch. "You're on, my man."

TD&D grinned. "And here I thought you didn't swing my way, what with you harassing Sonya and all."

The scarlet that erupted in Duane's cheeks almost made me laugh out loud. I held it in at the last moment. Revulsion pinched his face into an ugly mask of fear and prejudice.

"Hell no, man. I ain't like that," he spat.

"You're not saying there's something wrong with being gay, are you? Because if you are—"

"Oh come on, are we going to play darts or have a pissing match?" Duane's friend whined, sounding very uncomfortable with the turn of conversation.

TD&D laughed and slapped Duane on the shoulder, making him jump and stagger. "Relax. I was just messing with you."

The way Duane's face scrunched up made it look like he wanted to gnaw TD&D's hand off. Considering TD&D had at least thirty pounds of muscle on Duane, it looked like that would be a bad idea. But common sense—or really sense of any kind—wasn't Duane's thing. The nervous way Duane's friend danced from foot to foot and kept eyeing the exit revealed that he might have sense enough for both of them. A wicked thread deep inside me wanted to see Duane and TD&D go at it. The side of me that toiled not so tirelessly at becoming a doctor raged against the idiots actually wanting to hurt each other. They both postured for a second, chests puffing up, eyes locking with intent despite the smile on TD&D's face.

That smile became genuine and too gorgeous for my own good as it turned on me. "I'm coming back to find out where that trail is," he said.

The power of those captivating eyes of his made my blood pump to my cheeks and heat my skin with what was no doubt a bright pink blush. Smiling against my will, I shook my head and moved to a patron down the bar who hollered for another round. A guy with a gaze that stunning was bad news and that was the last thing I needed right now. The first thing I needed was good tips to help take the edge of the gargantuan student loans that had forced me to take the semester off. I put my cheeriest game face on and got to work.

While I slung drinks to the leering cowboys in their designer hats and cowgirls in their blingy boots that had never seen a drop of cow shit, I watched TD&D. From the bits I occasionally heard over the noise of the bar, they chipped at and teased one another. After a few minutes, though, it became good-natured. Soon they were laughing and slapping one another on the back as they shared tips and tricks for throwing darts. It was all TD&D. He had a way about him that put them at ease, made them laugh, hell, a magnetism that made them want to be around him. And they weren't the only ones.

Women in their painted-on jeans immediately flocked to the group, cheering TD&D on, pawing at him every time he stepped back to give one of the other guys a turn at throwing. He evaded them with what looked like practiced ease, positioning himself with a stool or a table between them. Though he smiled and spoke polite words to them, his gaze kept returning to me. I didn't want to be flattered by the fact that he ignored a leggy blond beautiful enough to grace the header of a fashion website. Instead, he watched little old me who looked like I'd walked out of the ghetto of a reservation. He could just be one of those guys that had a fetish about Native women. But it wasn't sexual fantasy lust I saw in his eyes; it was actual interest.

By the time they finished their dart game, the guys parted like old friends who couldn't wait to get back together again. Duane and his friend sauntered off to a recently vacated table and TD&D made his way up to the bar. Every stool was occupied, but he managed to slip between two patrons with a smile and a few polite words. Our gazes locked and warmth spread through me. Grinning like a teenager with a crush, I gravitated toward him.

I leaned over the bar so I wouldn't have to shout. And, I couldn't lie to myself; I wanted to be closer to him. "That was impressive," I said.

One eyebrow rose. "The dart game?"

"Yes, but not that. The way you went from a claws-out pissing match to being best buds with those guys. Not many could have done that, let alone would have bothered trying."

Eyes casting down, shoulders going up in a shrug, he smiled all demure like, and dammit if it wasn't cute as hell. "My father taught me fighting should always be a last resort."

"Sounds like you have a wise dad."

The smile morphed into a serious look. "I do."

Someone called for a drink down the bar. This time I didn't want the excuse to stop talking to TD&D. But, tips paid the bills. Shooting him an apologetic smile, I started down the bar. His hand shot out and covered mine. He turned my hand over and placed something in it; a note with a phone number on it.

"No pressure, but I'd love it if you could show me that trail," he said.

The way those gorgeous eyes pleaded with me from under his dark brows made my insides want to melt. He didn't seem at all like the bad news I'd thought he was when he first walked in. What would it hurt?

"How do I know you're not a serial killer or something trying to get me alone in the woods?" I half teased.

He laughed. "You don't, but I have a feeling you can take care of yourself."

That definitely charmed the pants off me. Little did he know I was a med student who would capture a spider and take it outside rather than kill it. But I liked that he didn't underestimate me just because I was a woman, and that he was willing to say so in front of the whole bar.

He gestured to the people in the bar. "Besides, we have all these witnesses that know I asked you to take me there."

Lips pursed, I nodded. "If I choose to dial these digits, what do I call you?"

His smile became radiant. Before that moment, I never would have thought of a man's smile as radiant, but damn it all if his wasn't enough to outshine the sun. The heat it put out could be downright dangerous.

"Raul. Raul Anderson."

"Raul?" I asked to make sure I'd heard him right. He nodded. "Okay, Raul. You're on. I'm Sonya."

His eyes closed for a moment like someone savoring a great piece of chocolate. "Sonya, I look forward to hearing from you." The way he said my name made my vulva muscles dance.

And just like that, I knew it was a bad idea. But, I also knew I'd be making that phone call.

CHAPTER TWO

RAUL

That woman was just too sexy for my own good. I needed to run like a running back playing for the pros; in more ways than one, but only one was an option. After a restless night at the winery B&B just outside of Twin Falls, breakfast, and a few hours waiting for my phone to ring, I drove way up into the Sawtooth mountains. My skin itched from the inside out with the desire to shift into wolf form and blow off this energy. But that hadn't been an option back in Twin Falls. The parks in town were small and hedged in with agricultural fields and residential areas. According to the brochures in the foyer of the B&B, there were plenty of waterfalls and hiking trails around. Problem was, there were plenty of people around too.

So, a long drive to the rarely used forest roads deep in the mountain it was. As a ranger for the state of Montana, I knew just where to find the best places, those roads abandoned by the state because they didn't have the money for their upkeep. Idaho was no different. The amount of dust on my black Porsche made me wish I'd brought my dual sport motorcycle instead. A twinge of guilt dug at me for getting such a beautiful car dirty. I probably should have rented a Jeep, but that would have felt too much like my work vehicle, and I just couldn't stomach how slow they drove.

Evergreen trees swallowed the road ahead, stretching up toward the blue sky. Dust motes filled the golden-hued early evening air. It had taken three hours and as many forestry roads to get deep enough into the mountains to reach somewhere secluded. I stepped off the overgrown dirt road into knee-high grass. The greedy gulp of mountain air I took filled my lungs to capacity. It tasted sweet, like pine trees and freedom.

I left my jacket and boots in the car, locked it out of habit even though there wasn't a human soul around for miles, and started off into the thick trees. The cool shade welcomed me by raising bumps along my skin. It wasn't cold that caused the reaction—even though it was less than sixty on a summer day—but anticipation. My kind didn't get cold very easily. A good distance from the car, I found a fir tree with boughs that swept the grass. I stripped completely and hid my clothes beneath it. Mountain air tickled along my exposed skin, making my balls tighten.

I called my wolf up. My skin warmed slightly as my body vibrated and atoms flowed. A second later my paws hit the ground and the world exploded into a million different scents. I shook from my nose to my tail, twisting my neck in the back and forth motion that moved every strand of grey, white, and black hair. Blinking to adjust my brain to the world becoming shades of red and blue, I suppressed a howl of celebration. It would be dangerous to attract that kind of attention. Even when times were good, too many people killed wolves on sight, some to protect their livestock, some out of fear, and the worst did it just for sport. But times were far from good. Wolf attacks were on the rise so much that they made the news weekly. And they weren't on livestock, they were on people, which was exactly what had brought me to Twin Falls, Idaho.

Trotting off into the trees, I lifted my nose in the air and breathed deep to get the lay of the land. Web on top of intricate web of scent trails stretched out in front of me. Some promised to lead down literal rabbit holes, some metaphorical ones. Since I knew I wouldn't find wolves this close to even an unused forest road, I followed a deer trail. It eventually led to the trail of a small herd. This trail led me deep into the shade of the thick forest. Soon the clean, slightly metallic scent of a stream came upon the breeze. A mile or so later my paws carried me to a silver ribbon of water no more than a foot-wide winding its way over tumbled rocks.

The scents of dozens of creatures spread out from this area. Among them, I smelled wolf, normal wolf. I followed the trail, my paw prints covering theirs at times and dwarfing them. Signs of their presence started to pop up; tufts of hair here, a paw print there. As I got deeper into the forest, a variety of pine and fir trees competed for space, creating enough shade that the sun only touched my back occasionally. I wove through the numerous trunks, ducking and dodging around low branches like a field of linebackers. Part of the reason I loved running so much was because it reminded my human side of my days on the football field. Those days had been less complicated, Hel, the world had been less complicated then.

Paw prints started to show up everywhere in the dirt and forest duff. The scent of more than half a dozen wolves filled the air. I slowed as the scent trails grew newer and fresher. Flanking them, I scanned the rocky forest with my sharpened vision. My nose told me their scents concentrated about a half mile up ahead to the northeast. That direction grew rockier, which could mean caves, dens. Giving it a wide birth, I headed downwind, skirting around through the thick trees. On a hill a little over a half mile or so away, I spotted them.

A group of gray wolves lounged in the sun on a rock outcropping surrounded by trees. The darkness of a large cave yawned behind them. From what I could see and smell, it was two adult females, a male, and a pair of cubs that were a few months old. They appeared to be of a healthy weight, coats glossy and full. Another adult male lay a short distance away, enduring the attentions of a slightly older pup who crawled all over him and tugged at his ears with his teeth. Relief swelled within at seeing even this small pack healthy, happy, and relatively safe.

I mentally cataloged their individual markings and characteristics for later recording. A new pack to add to my catalog always sent a thrill through me. This pack would be number nine in my book of four states and two provinces of Canada that I had visited.

As much as I wanted to stay, I didn't dare. The sun wouldn't be up much longer, which meant they'd be on the move to go hunting. If they came across me it could spook them. I didn't want to give them any reason to move on from this place. It was as safe as a place could be, far from humans and their livestock, nowhere near any popular hiking areas, and abundant with wildlife. Safe places were hard to come by for a wolf pack of any size, and I wouldn't be the one to take that away from them. I crept back slowly, careful not to rub against any underbrush that would capture pieces of my fur and leave behind more of my scent.

Satisfied with a day that was successful in so many ways, my mouth spread into a wolfy grin as I trotted back toward the car. Twilight turned the forest shades of gold that reminded me of Sonya's eyes. They had been captivating. Even with a rocking body that would make a college cheerleader jealous, those eyes had held my attention. If only she knew how special she was. Would she be different once she found out? Damn, that woman was distracting. I sped my pace up. The thoughts melted away as I fell into the rhythm of running. Exercise cleansed my mind, focused me, even more so when in wolf form. All that mattered was the forest floor beneath my paws and the fading sunlight on my fur.

On a rocky ridge a few miles from the car, I caught scent of something that stopped me in my tracks. Claws scraped against granite as I skidded. Every muscle tense, I sniffed the air, turning my head this way and that to catch it once again. From the east, I picked it up. Werewolf. And a familiar one at that. Tyler Viðarrson. I hadn't thought his territory extended this far west, but clearly, I'd been wrong. This would complicate things. I had to get close to Sonya sooner rather than later. Dammit.

Turning tail, I launched into an all-out run toward the car, treating it like the goal line at a Bowl game. Every moment I was out here I risked running into him, and he was definitely in my top two of people I never wanted to encounter again. He could screw everything up. At my clothes, I shifted back to human form. I dressed as I continued the jog to the car. Once inside, I fired it up, shifted into reverse, and flew down the dirt road in reverse. Half a mile later, I came to a grassy spot wide enough to whip the Porsche around. As I shifted into first, the car dinged, telling me I had a voicemail on my phone. I commanded it to play the message.

"All right, Raul, you're on. Tomorrow morning, 5:00AM, meet me in the bar parking lot. Bring your best pair of shoes and water to drink. If you don't show, don't bother to try again," Sonya's beautiful, alto voice heavy with challenge came through the car's speakers.

"Return text," I told the car.

I shifted into second, barreling down the rough dirt road far faster than was good for the Porsche's suspension.

"I'll be there."

CHAPTER THREE

SONYA

Dorothy's powerhouse blues-rock voice singing about how a man could "Kiss It" was still fading from the speakers of my black Jeep CJ when another vehicle pulled into the empty bar parking lot. I think it was a newer black Porsche, though it was hard to tell through the layers of dust that concealed the poor thing. Behind the washer-fluid streaked windshield I spotted Raul's scruffily handsome face and striking brown eyes with gold flecks throughout. He was on-time to the point of almost beating me; that was a first. I couldn't help but be a bit impressed.

I hopped out of my Jeep, tossed my long, windblown braid of hair over my shoulder, and leaned back against the driver side rock bar. My gaze skimmed the Porsche. The Montana license plate read 4THAN11. I suspected it was personalized, but I had no idea what it meant.

I crossed my arms beneath my breasts, which were already lifted to an impressive shelf thanks to the lacy push-up bra. My black V-neck tee from *The Pretty Reckless* concert revealed just enough cleavage to be what I considered a touch risky. The loose blue jeans and well-worn hiking boots probably counteracted that, but hey, we were going hiking, and I was nothing if not practical. Well, practical to a point. A girl had to look good on a not-date, hence the push-up bra.

A small dust cloud rose into the dawn light when he shut the Porsche's door. He stepped away smooth and lightning fast, fast enough that not even a speck of that dust touched his long sleeve, silky green, button-up shirt. Blue jeans so dark they looked brand new hugged his fit legs, butt, and crotch in all the right places. From the perfect lines of his carefully manicured five-o'clock shadow to his spotless hiking boots, everything about him looked designer. And was that hair product in his brown-black hair making it look like a stylish mess? Surely he didn't just wake up that way. I couldn't smell any product or cologne, and I had a hell of a sense of smell compared to most. I liked that he didn't feel the need to drown in a scent that wasn't his own body chemistry.

His eyes drank me in from the toes of my hiking boots to the long, black braid of my hair. Desire flared in them.

"Good morning," he said through a smile that could stop traffic. A nice rumble punctuated his low voice, making a tingle spread through me. Yep, that voice was just as sexy and masculine as I remembered.

I pulled out my phone and snapped a picture of him. "Good morning," I replied, and meant it. It wasn't every morning I got to go hiking with a sexy stranger, which was why I had told one of the waitresses at the bar exactly where I was going and with who. While he gave me a querulous look, I texted the waitress his picture.

"Not that I mind, but why the pic?" he asked.

I looked him square in the eyes as I answered to better judge his reaction. "So my co-worker will know who to send the cops after if I don't come back."

He laughed, a deep, genuine sound that rumbled as much as his voice and vibrated along my skin. Heated blood worked its way to my breasts and groin.

"Smart and beautiful. I admire that," he said. His gaze traveled past me to my Jeep.

I stiffened, preparing to defend her; she was being restored on a college student budget, and he had pulled up in a sports car after all.

"Black on black, hum? You even powder coated all the chrome bits," he observed in a non-judgmental tone.

"Yep." My gaze flicked to his car. "Flashy isn't my thing."

He walked around it, making appreciative noises as he passed the

Smittybilt winch and custom bumpers. "You in the process of having it restored?"

"Of doing it myself, yep."

His brows rose as he straightened and looked at me. "Yourself?"

"Yep," I said again.

One corner of his lip quirked up and he tugged the other between his teeth in an expression that revealed his desire. "Nice," he said in a breathy voice.

The fact that he was impressed by me doing my own mechanical work didn't impress me. Most guys liked it at first. It fed some kind of fantasy they had of a greasy girl with tools in her hands. But then they realized it meant I spent a lot of time actually working on my rig instead of focusing on them. Their fascination faded quickly after that.

"Are you a mechanic?" Raul asked.

"Nope, just a starving medical student." I decided not to mention having to take the semester off because I was broke and drowning in student loans.

"That makes sense."

It was my turn to raise a brow at him. "Really? That's the opposite of what most people say."

He shrugged. "Both professions have outstanding hand-eye coordination and understand how machines work."

I tried hard not to be too impressed, too interested in him, but he was doing an excellent job of knocking down my defenses. Now came the next test.

I motioned to the Jeep with an inclination of my head. "Hop in. Your car will never make it up the road we're going on."

One brow rising, he stood a bit taller as if squaring off with my Jeep.

"Afraid you'll mess up your perfectly mussed hair?" I teased, inclining my head toward the topless Jeep.

A short laugh escaped him. "Hardly. I love the wind in my hair. My motorcycle jacket isn't just for show." He strode up to the Jeep and jumped in.

That made things down low tingle. Swallowing my libido, I climbed in and put my seatbelt on. I waited. We shared a long look before he shook his head as if surprised he forgot, then put his seatbelt on. It made me wonder if he was reckless enough not to typically wear one, or if my Jeep and I had flustered him that much. His brow went back up as he watched me grab the flathead screwdriver from the console and use it to turn the ignition over. Contrary to how that looked, the Jeep purred to life with a nice little rumble that betrayed the high-end motor and new exhaust I'd put in. I'd turned the radio off before getting out earlier, so the only sound was the engine.

He smiled and nodded. "Small but mighty," he said with appreciation.

From the way he looked at me when he said it, I wasn't sure if he meant the Jeep, me, or both. Either way, I liked it.

"What does 4th and eleven mean?" I asked with a thrust of my head in the direction of his car.

"It's actually 4th and inches. It's part of a football saying '4th and inches, do you have what it takes'. It's about putting it all on the line, committing to the goal as a team."

While he'd lost me at "football saying," I liked the sound of his voice enough that a smile came easily to my lips. In the close proximity of the vehicle his scent wrapped around me like the arms of a warm, woodsy embrace. It lacked the sweet, fake smell of cologne, though. He smelled more like he had stepped out of a forest instead of a dusty sports car. Something in me stirred at it, and I wasn't sure if it was desire or something else. A bit flustered and liking it, I put the Jeep in first gear and focused on the road.

"So, what do you do for a living, Raul?" I asked to fill the silence.

"I'm a forest ranger."

Jaw dropping, I gave him a long look. "For real?"

The motorcycle jacket with biker gang-like rockers and a wicked cool Norse knot wolf's head on the back that he'd worn last night, designer clothes, the sports car, none of it added up to forest ranger.

"For real," he said in all seriousness.

Well, it would explain the forest smell that clung to him as if it were his natural scent, and possibly the wolf's head on his jacket. Maybe he wasn't the bad boy I'd thought he was last night when he walked into the bar. But what kind of a forest ranger could catch a dart in mid-air, then throw it and land it right in the bull's eye without looking at the board? That spoke more of ex-military or some other highly trained and very dangerous kind of profession.

"What made you want to get into forestry?" I tested, trying to sound conversational rather than like I was psychoanalyzing him.

"Preservation. The more we know about the forests, the better our chances of saving them, and the animals that live in them."

I took my eyes off the road completely for a moment to look at him straight on. His face looked as sincere as his voice had sounded, but the bad boy vibe resonated through him. It didn't make sense.

"You're surprised?" he asked.

"Um...uh...well, yeah," I admitted, not knowing what else to say.

Instead of elaborating, he turned the tide on me. "What made you want to be a doctor?"

"I want to help people."

"And you will." He said with complete confidence as if he could see the future. It made me smile. "So, a doctor who hikes, huh?"

"Yep. Nature grounds me, helps me make sense of the world."

He turned toward me as much as his seatbelt would allow. "Really?"

I made an affirmative humming noise. "Always has. At least, ever since I can remember. My parents took me hiking and camping a lot when I was a kid. They loved the outdoors, and it made me love it too." The memory hurt, but it also made me smile. I didn't want to get all emotional on a first date, so I changed the subject.

"Raul is an interesting name."

His perfectly landscaped scruffy cheeks moved up in the beginnings of a smile, but didn't quite make it all the way. "It's a variance of the ancient Germanic name Radulf, though my parents changed the spelling to be more English friendly, so it reads more like the Spanish version."

"Are your ancestors German?"

"Icelandic."

I hadn't seen that one coming. "Cool." The instant reaction made me want to bury my head in sand. Cool, really? Ugh.

"What about you? Sonya is Russian, isn't it? Yet you look at least part Native American."

Long black hair, tanned brown skin, it wasn't a stretch that he'd figured that part out. "You're close. My mom is full-blooded Cherokee and my dad was Swedish-American. His parents were from Sweden."

"Wow. Now that is cool."

His play on my own words almost made me laugh. But I couldn't laugh after mentioning my dad. The pain was too much. The oddness of him having descended from the same culture as my dad's family took some of the edge off. It wasn't often I met someone of Scandinavian descent.

I turned onto Rock Creek Road leading up Pike Mountain to the ski area. Grass covered hills dotted with flowering bushes stretched out around us.

"Have you been to Sweden?" he asked.

"A few times when I was young. We visited relatives in Stockholm and went and saw Gamla Stan." I remembered how excited my dad had been to visit his parents' homeland. That did make me smile, even though it hurt. I had to get him off the subject before this date took a weepy turn that would ensure there wouldn't be a second. "What about you, ever been to Iceland?"

"My parents took me every summer until I turned sixteen."

Was that a touch of bitterness in his voice? "I hear it's beautiful, all waterfalls and glaciers."

A huge smile spread across his face, banishing all traces of tightness in his features. He lit up as he delved into a description of all the waterfalls and the amazing hiking trails. Seeing the rugged, beautiful land through his eyes made me want to go there. His love for the land shone through his exuberant tone and his words about packing things in and out, leaving them better than one found them, and the gentle way he spoke of the creatures he encountered. My original impression of him being a bad boy melted more with each word. It had been a front, a shield he put up to keep certain people at a distance and give the appearance of strength. What in his life made him feel the need to exude such strength?

I tried my best to shut my budding psychologist's mind off. It would be best if he didn't realize what kind of doctor I wanted to be right away. Most guys ran for the hills once they figured out I was more interested in exploring the mind than cutting up the body. Go figure.

"I'm talking way too much. So what about you, do you like to travel?" he asked.

"I love it. I wish I had the chance to do more of it."

He nodded in understanding. "School makes it so hard. When I was in college I didn't have the time to go anywhere."

That got us off onto a tangent about college that left us laughing so hard the tears in my eyes made me hit more than one rut in the road leftover from the snowplows. Raul grabbed the roll bar as we bounced along and laughed even harder. We talked about the places we wanted to visit and I was surprised to find his list was almost as long as mine. He seemed far less passionate about it, like it was something he would like to do, but didn't felt compelled to do like I did. But then, I'd found most people didn't have the travel bug nearly as bad as me.

"Someday I want to travel all over, see the world and all the different people in it," I said.

"And you will," he said with complete confidence.

I laughed, but it was a bitter sound. "Yeah, maybe in twenty years when I'm no longer buried under student loans."

I turned off the pavement onto a rough dirt road, but instead of continuing up it, I pulled the Jeep off to the side and shut the engine off.

One eyebrow quirked up, Raul looked at me. "What, afraid this beast can't make it up?"

I patted the dashboard. "She can definitely make it up, but that takes half the fun out of it and shortens the hike."

"I like how you think."

Relief eased muscles I hadn't realized had tensed. Part of me had been afraid he wasn't much of a hiker. Sure, he said he was a forest ranger, but with the car and the clothes, I wasn't quite convinced yet. That was why the lipstick in my front pocket was actually bear spray in disguise, a little thing my dad had gotten me in the habit of carrying when I'd started dating in high school. It hadn't been cleverly disguised back then. Nowadays, websites like Women on Guard made self-defense discreet and stylish at the same time. Not that I thought I'd have to use it on Raul, he didn't give off those vibes. But one couldn't be careful enough when taking a guy they'd just met at a bar out into the mountains alone.

I hopped out of the rig, shut the door, and pocketed my cell phone—which had no service up here at all—on the side opposite my pepper spray lipstick. I shrugged into a light pack filled with only snacks, water, and a rudimentary first aid kit. Raul came around the Jeep to stand beside me, looking as perfect as he had before stepping into my Jeep. Few people I'd met could pull off the windblown look and make it that sexy. Numerous strands of my black hair had come loose from my braid, no doubt making me look a bit of a mess. Though I knew my face hid my emotions perfectly —a thing I had honed over the years—he smiled as if he could sense my arousal.

"All right, poster boy, let's see if you can hike," I said.

That handsome face split into a grin. "Poster boy?"

Starting up the hill, I shot him a side glance. "Yep, like one of those models for the clothing stores or fragrances: perfect clothes, perfect hair, perfect face."

He wiggled his brows at me. "Perfect, huh?"

Laughing, I bumped his shoulder with mine. Warmth radiated from him so powerfully that I felt it through both of our shirts. "Careful, if you get cerebral edema, you won't look so perfect."

A low sound between a growl and a hum came from him. "It's very sexy when you use doctor jargon," he said.

"I'm sure you could match me with forestry jargon."

As we hiked along the ever-steepening trail, he pointed to a tall pine tree to our right. "Pseudotsuga menziesii of the Pinaceae family, which doesn't produce seeds until it reaches the age of twenty-five."

"Wow, that is sexy. And I never knew Douglas fir trees were so responsible as not to reproduce until they reached twenty-five," I teased.

A grin handsome enough to make my breath catch turned up the manscaped edges of his perfectly maintained five o'clock shadow. He pointed to a grove of aspen trees clustered in a cleft between hills. "And that is Populus tremuloides, which has a deceptive reproduction system. It looks like there are many in that grove, doesn't it?"

I nodded and made an affirmative noise.

He went on. "There really isn't. They are all clones of the same tree, part of its roots, and in essence, kind of the same tree. The female tree, or grove, requires pollination from the male before releasing her seeds, and a male could be miles away in another grove of his own making. Otherwise, they can never spread beyond their own damp area."

"Interesting," I drew the word out, unsure of whether or not it really was.

He laughed. "Tragically romantic in a way, if you think about it. They need one another if they are ever going to spread their wings and expand beyond their corner of the world."

That made me look at him hard and see something much more than just a handsome face. At my encouragement, he delved into a description of a wildflower, then a bush. He interjected his own quirky little fact with a clever comment after each one. The man clearly had a brain bigger than the bulge in his jeans and was kind of funny to boot. Handsome and a sense of humor was a dangerous combination. By the time we got to the top of the Jeep road, my sides hurt from laughing much more than they did from the hike.

We paused in silence at the top, taking in the view of rolling hills of grass and fragrant wildflowers topped with a cloudless blue sky. I drew in a long breath of the perfect air. Contrary to the old cliche, a vista like this gave me breath instead of taking it away. I removed my pack, took my water bottle from it, and swallowed a long drink. Raul did a slow, small circle, taking in the views with a huge grin on his face. The golden light of that magical hour just after dawn illuminated him, and suddenly the view was literally breathtaking.

"It's beautiful here. Not as forested as I like, but beautiful. Do you come here often?" he asked.

"A bit late for pickup lines, don't you think?"

He chuckled, a carefree sound that sent tingles through me. "I'm not one for pickup lines."

Gaze traveling the length of his body, I forced myself to breathe. "I don't imagine you need to be." I cleared my throat and answered his question. "I'm more of a grease-under-my-fingernails kind of girl than a dirt-on-my-shoes kind of girl, but yeah. I try to hike at least once a week. It's good for the psyche." Once a week, although nowhere near the forest. But I wasn't about to say that part. Then I'd have to explain how the forest made me miss my dad, and how it made me feel like a powder keg in a burning building.

"Ah, I was right then."

Dread filled me. I tried to sound light-hearted as I asked. "About what?"

He said the words that usually meant the date was over and there wouldn't be another one. "You're studying psychology, not medicine."

Bummer. I had started to like this one.

Then he said something that threw me for a loop. "That makes sense."

"How so?"

A rush of blood turned his cheeks pink, and he started to stutter. Or, he could have been choking. It was hard to tell by the sounds he made. "Um, uh, I only meant that you're good with people, being a bartender and all, and you seem to like people. So it makes sense."

I handed him my water bottle. He took a long drink before handing it back with a grateful smile. His embarrassment was cute, odd, but cute. And, the reaction was so different from what I'd expected that I smiled back at him. He wasn't running off into the hills, so that was a good thing.

"Well, I've only recently switched my focus. The problem with going to college is that when you start, you have no idea what you want in life."

"Isn't that the truth," he said with a long sigh as he sat down on a rock. His eyes beckoned with a look between me and the rock. I sat down beside him, close enough that our thighs touched. The heat of his skin burned right through my jeans in a delicious way.

"You didn't go straight into forestry?"

Caution filled his eyes as he looked long and hard at me. "I don't usually tell women this on the first date because they either run screaming or fangirl."

When he didn't go on, I gave him an expectant look.

"I got in on a football scholarship and planned to just go for a Bachelor of Arts while focusing on football."

My brows rose. Given his muscles, height, and athletic ability to hike up that hill without breaking even the tiniest sweat, it made sense. "Which reaction do you prefer?"

His expression fell into one that mirrored the dread I'd felt earlier. "Neither. I love the game, and I always will, but it doesn't define me, and I don't want people to think it does."

He handed my water bottle back and I let my fingers linger on his for a long moment. "You're kind of wise. Would it crush you if I said I don't care for football?"

Making a sound of pain, he clutched his chest. "A little."

Not caring about potentially getting his germs, I took another drink before responding. "I don't hate it, but I don't really get the draw either."

"It's the teamwork, the way eleven men work so hard together to achieve a goal, just for the fun of it, how good it feels to know you've successfully led them to that goal."

"Ahhh, you were the quarterback."

He groaned, tension pulling his back up straight. "Don't look at me that way! It's not what you think. I'm not a glory hound."

I bumped my shoulder into his and gave him a playful smile. "I don't think that. I was just messing with you. I can tell by the way you talk, the look in your eyes, that it's about the team."

A long breath eased from him. I stood, offering him my hand. He took it and let me help him to his feet. The way he unfolded over me, all tall muscle, made me a bit weak in the knees. And he lingered, hovering over me a mere foot away, his body heat and forest smell wrapping around me. His hand scorched mine. Either the hike had gotten to him more than it seemed, or he was getting hot for me. I hoped it was the latter. And I hoped he didn't let go.

The urge to touch his chest, feel if it was as hard as it looked, had me lifting my other hand before I knew what I was doing. Why not? It seemed like he hadn't enticed me up here to kill me after all. And the guy was hot as all hell. Just before I made contact, voices drifted to us on the morning breeze. I dropped my hand, pulled my other free of his, and stepped back.

We shared a secret smile just before a couple and their massive German Shepard crested the hill. Fan-like tail wagging, tongue lolling out the side of his mouth, the dog bounded to us. Twenty feet from us he skidded to a halt, tucked his tail, and hunched down as if afraid. His big brown eyes were locked on Raul. The couple was so busy taking in the view, they didn't even notice their dog's reaction. Walking on without him, and ignoring us, they oohed and ahhed, and half-hugged each other. They didn't quite give off an anti-social vibe. They were part of the cell-phone-captivated generation from what I guessed of their ages. It was almost always like this when I came across their kind on the trails. They would find anything else to look at so they didn't have to interact with a person outside of their circle.

An entire field of psychological study on that alone was rising.

Raul crouched, inclined his head, and extended his hand to the dog. He looked back and forth between his people and Raul a few times before inching forward slowly. As the dog grew closer, he slinked down onto his belly and scooted forward the last few feet. Head on the ground, he rolled over and exposed his belly. The dog's people still hadn't noticed. Speaking soft words to him, Raul scratched his belly until his tail started to wag.

"Oh my goodness! I am so sorry! He didn't bite you, did he?" a woman's voice preceded the crunch of gravel as she approached.

The dog flipped over but remained laying by Raul's side.

"No, no. He just wanted a belly rub. He was a good dog." Raul said the last bit to the dog in a soft voice filled with praise. The dog's tail wagged harder as he looked up at Raul with what I could only call adoration.

"What?" the woman sounded confused.

"Sampson! Get over here! What are you doing?" the man demanded of the dog, who didn't move.

"Sampson, now!" the man demanded in a tone that made me bristle.

Sampson stood, licked Raul's hand, and trotted over to his master. The man proceeded to tell him what a bad dog he was in a horrible, condescending voice. I ground my teeth together to keep from interjecting.

Raul took a step in the couple's direction. "Really, it's not his fault. All dogs love me, I just have a way with them."

The man made a snorting noise as he shot Raul a piercing glare that only made him stand a bit taller. While they likely weighed about the same, Raul looked like he had sixty pounds of muscle where the other man was doughy. But having the dog at his side seemed to bolster his confidence. He stood taller, still several inches short of Raul's six-two.

"Yes, and I'm sure there are serial killers that are great with some dogs too. Which makes him pretty useless as a guard dog for my wife," the man snapped.

The petite woman looked like she wanted to melt into the knee-high grass and disappear. Her gaze looked anywhere but at us or her husband. The man turned and began to storm away, tugging his wife after him by the arm. Sampson turned back to look at Raul. Making a horrible imitation of a growl, the man reached back, grabbed Sampson by the collar, and yanked him after them.

"Come on, dog. It's time we took a little trip to the pound to trade you for something that will do its job."

Something that sounded like a real growl came from Raul. He moved in the man's direction but stopped when I put a hand on his arm. "He's just embarrassed that his dog likes you better. He'll probably get over it by the time they get home," I whispered.

Though he didn't call after them, or take another step, he watched until they descended out of sight. He turned to me with a half-smile. "Sorry, I can't stand it when people are mean to animals."

I waved a hand. "He was just posturing, don't sweat it."

"Yeah, you're probably right." He didn't look or sound convinced, and the way he kept glancing back the direction the couple had gone made me think he wanted to follow them to make sure the guy wasn't mean to the dog.

This one could prove to be a keeper. "Hey, how about I treat you to lunch and you can tell me more about Iceland?" I asked, trying to look enticing despite being covered in dust and pollen.

The gorgeous smile that spread across his lips made me feel even frumpier. But I didn't care, because it was directed at me.

"I'd like that. But I wouldn't be much of a gentleman if I let you treat me."

We started back down the hillside together. I let out a short laugh. "One, I am not some old-fashioned damsel. Two, we'll see if you think it's a treat after you taste my cooking. How does a picnic in the park sound?"

"Sounds great, so long as I'm not stealing too much of your time."

I found myself staring at his canines. The guy had four canine-like teeth that came to slight points where most people only had two. It was hard to tell unless you were really looking, but the way he kept smiling, I couldn't help but notice. I couldn't decide if it was sexy or slightly disturbing. The muscles tightening between my legs made it clear my body was deciding on the sexy side. Most people would have allowed their orthodontist to file those teeth down. I liked that he hadn't felt the need to alter his body to conform to societal expectations. It pointed to a healthy self-confidence.

It hit me that I had been so focused on his devilish good looks that I hadn't answered his question. Ignoring the heat rushing to my face, I said, "It isn't stealing if I give it to you. Are you up for doing the hiking loop to the ski hill parking lot first?"

"Hell yeah," he said through a grin that made me want to crawl all over him instead of psychoanalyze him.

My heart sped up. Grinning like a fool, I led the way down the path.

While he may not have come out here to kill me and leave my body in the mountains, he was certainly still dangerous. This was a danger I was eager to explore.

CHAPTER FOUR

RAUL

Tonight I had to broach the unbroachable subject. Last weekend's amazing time hiking and picnicking made me long to take things slow with Sonya. She was special, and not just because of what she would be to all of my kind. But I had no choice. A quick trip home last Wednesday to check on my sister and get fresh clothes had only left me feeling more anxious.

I parked my freshly washed Hayabusa motorcycle next to her Jeep and stepped out into the thick darkness of a cloudy night. Hot as it was tonight, I figured she might like a bit more wind in her hair, so long as the extra helmet I had strapped to the tiny passenger seat fit her. Hanging my own helmet on the license plate hanger, I ran my fingers through my hair to liven it back up. A glance in the left handlebar mirror showed my brown and black locks to be rakish enough to be considered handsome. I hoped. At least it was better than helmet hair.

The black ribbon of a walkway between two apartment buildings unfolded into a yawning darkness. Behind me the dull yellow streetlight flickered from the wings of at least a dozen moths. Even above the scent of some nearby rosebushes, a freshly cut lawn, and a few dogs, I smelled Sonja. My wolf eyes adjusted in a blink as I stepped into the yawning darkness created by the buildings.

The scent of roses made me smile. I had dinner at the bar each night this last week with the excuse they had the best burgers in town—which they did. But, the real reason had been so I could see Sonya. Monday night I had left a white rose tucked under the windshield wiper of her Jeep, Tuesday a yellow one, Wednesday a pink one. The one question I was looking forward to asking her tonight was which was her favorite.

The clop of my boots against the sidewalk echoed down the walkway between buildings. Part of me liked that she trusted me enough to let me pick her up at her apartment. Another part felt a painful twinge of guilt because of the false pretenses we were starting this whole relationship on. Determined not to overthink it, I shoved the thoughts down.

Through all the other domestic sounds, I heard her soft footsteps within her apartment, followed by the jingle of her keys as she made her way to the door. Anticipation shot through me. False pretenses or not, I liked her, a lot. Straightening the collar of my forest green, button up, silk shirt, I stopped in front of her door. I'd chosen my custom fit black leather jacket to go over my clothes instead of the Cordura one. It still sported my rockers and the knotwork wolf's head on the back, but the expensive cut and leather had a dressy look to it. Sonya deserved dressy.

Knowing she was about to open the door, I waited, hands in my pockets. She jumped a bit at the sight of me, but the surprised "O" her red lips made relaxed quickly into a smile. Smokey eye shadow made her topaz eyes stand out like shining gems. A lacy, grey and midnight blue striped shirt wrapped around her in soft layers, crossing low enough over her breasts to expose a tantalizing amount of cleavage. Black jeans hugged her slender legs and disappeared into nearly knee-high black boots.

A growling sound of approval slid from me. I dragged my gaze up to her face and the delicious blush reddening her cheeks made me sorry my attention had strayed. Desire darkened her eyes to a burnished gold. My blood heated.

"Wow," she said through a breath. The sound made more than my blood heat. "I am really underdressed."

I shook my head. "No way. You look amazing."

Eyes rolling skyward, she pulled the door closed and locked it. "Target sales rack compared to Saks," she murmured so quiet it was clear she didn't intend for me to hear.

I moved close enough that she had to put a hand against my chest to keep from falling into me when she turned around. Taking advantage of the situation, I place a hand on each of her shoulders to steady her. "I mean it. You could stop traffic, and you'd do it with ease, while I had to resort to designers to make me look this good."

An easy, natural laugh came from her. "Round one to you," she teased. "Should I grab a jacket?"

"Definitely. Leather if you have it."

After a widening of her eyes, she ducked back into the apartment for a moment. When she came back out, she had on a worn-in, black, leather jacket that swallowed her up. The scent of leather that had seen a lot of road miles and been well cared for with regular conditioner clung to it. If I didn't know better, I would be afraid it was an old boyfriend's. But she didn't know that I knew better, and would likely think me creepy if she did, so I lifted my brows and put on a jealous look.

"A bit big on you," I said, adding a touch of fake jealousy to my tone.

A sad smile played at her lips as she pulled the door closed behind her, locked it, and put her keys in one of the deep pockets. "It was my dad's." The sadness in her voice made me feel terrible for making her say the words.

I put one hand on the small of her back as we started to walk, and leaned in close. "In that case, I guess I can't be jealous," I said, dropping my voice an octave or two.

She shivered a bit and moved closer. I let my arm slide around her, enjoying the warmth of her body pressed against mine despite the seventy plus degree night.

When she saw my bike basking in the light of the streetlamp next to her Jeep, her steps hesitated for a split second. "You're not afraid of motorcycles, are you?" I asked.

She blew air through her lips in a dismissive noise. "Of course not, my dad was a biker. I'm cautious of them and painfully aware of the multitude of ways one can get injured or killed on them." She sounded light-hearted about it, and I knew from my research that her dad hadn't died in a motorcycle crash. It had been something much more nefarious than even she knew about.

"Does this mean I'm going to have trouble convincing you to straddle one behind me?"

"Hell no. But you may get a rundown of the videos I had to watch in med school if you drive too crazy." The teasing tone of her voice made me smile.

"Fair enough."

We reached the parking lot and I retrieved two helmets from my bike. She gave me a satisfied nod.

"You're off to a good start with those," she said through a smile that made my jeans tight.

Holding the helmet between her knees, she wove her hair into a quick braid, tying it off with a hairband I hadn't seen on her wrist until that moment.

I gave her a crooked smile. "Always prepared, I like that."

"Girl Scout," she said with a lift of her chin.

"Really?" I asked, hoping my surprise didn't show too much. I hadn't read that in her file.

She shrugged one shoulder. "Well, if a single summer counts."

I swung a leg over the bike. "Totally does. Why only one summer?"

After putting her helmet on, she lifted the visor. "Promise you won't judge?"

"I never would."

I fired up the engine and patted the seat behind me. She climbed on and wrapped her arms around me without being prompted. That hot little body of hers burned against my back in more ways than one.

"I punched a girl for talking bad about my dad."

Laughter erupted from me as I pictured her as a little girl defending her dad's honor. "Good for you!"

A short laugh came from her and she leaned her head on my shoulder. "Mom didn't think so, and I wasn't allowed back in after that, but yeah, it was pretty awesome."

One of her hands left my middle to close her visor. When it returned, she gripped me all the tighter. Her soft curves threatened to burn a line right through both of our leather jackets. I eased the bike from the parking lot onto the empty two-lane road, giving Sonja a chance to get a feel for the movement of the bike. She molded to me like an expert, leaning when I leaned, keeping the distance between us closed. We wove our way through the quiet streets. I kept my speed down until the last light of town lay behind us. Warm summer wind whipped at us as I accelerated and shifted through the gears. Sonya pressed so close the heat between her legs burned my backside in a maddening way.

Soon, trees lined the road instead of buildings. Clean, country air poured down my throat. A few miles out of town I turned onto the side road that led to the winery bed and breakfast I was staying at. Lilac bushes competed with Aspen trees for space along the shoulder, filling the air with their sweet scent. The bike's headlight cut through the growing dark, messing with my wolf night vision and forcing me to rely on my human eyes. As much as I wanted to shut off the headlight, I had to keep up appearances for Sonya's sake. She wasn't ready for the truth yet, not by a long shot. Tonight I hoped to take a big step in the direction of preparing her.

A wooden sign over a wrought iron gate welcomed us to the winery and B&B. Like a second skin, Sonja leaned into the corners of the winding driveway with me. For an all new reason, I was glad the driveway was almost a mile long. Row after row of grapevines stretched out from each side of the road, reaching up and over the rolling hills. From a navy blue sky a three-quarter moon turned the grapevines silver. Though the grapes were just starting to grow, their sweet smell filled the air with mouthwatering promise.

The driveway split—one direction going to a drive that circled before the winery, the other leading around the back where the B&B entrance and restaurant lay. I took the one going around the back. Candlelight flickered from the lone table sitting on the cobblestone patio beneath a pergola dripping with grapevines and wisteria. A roaring fire in a stacked stone fire pit not twenty feet away added to the ambiance.

I pulled the bike into the empty little parking lot and balanced it while Sonja stepped off. Light glowed from the kitchen window not far away where a staff member bustled about. I removed my helmet and jacket, hanging the helmet on the handlebars and draping the jacket over my seat once I got off. Helmet in hand, Sonya took in the picturesque grounds as she smoothed her hair.

"Wow, this place is amazing," she murmured more to herself as she turned in a half circle.

The light from the house and nearby fire played across her curves as she turned. Thankfully, she spoke because all of a sudden, I had no words.

"The parking lot is empty. Are you the only one staying here?"

To give myself time to break free of my vocal paralysis, I took the helmet from her and hung it over the other handlebar. "Yeah. Everyone wants to be here during harvest season, which isn't until August or September, so I have the place to myself."

Wits finally about me again, I offered her my elbow. She looked down at it like she wasn't sure what to do with it, shook her head, laughed, then looped her arm through it. "I've never had a date offer me his elbow."

I led her toward the back patio. "I was raised with old fashioned values, some of which I actually like quite a bit."

Again she laughed, but it was a pleased sound. "Well careful, Raul Anderson. A girl could get used to this kind of treatment."

"So you're saying I'm already outshining your other dates?" I teased.

"Maybe," she said in a playful tone that told me I definitely was.

She fit nicely against my side, her high-heeled boots bringing her hip nearly level with mine. They had to be nearly four inches tall, considering I was six-four and she was around five-six. My mind couldn't stop going over the benefits of those four-inch heels. The darkness fell away the closer we got to the table, forcing me to slow and let my eyes adjust. It didn't hurt that it gave me more time to touch her soft skin and feel her body heat next to mine. The summer night was warm enough, but hers was a heat I wanted to bury myself in.

Forcing such thoughts to the back of my mind before they could go to the crotch of my jeans, I let go of her arm. I dashed ahead, pulled the chair out for her, and picked up the dozen red roses sitting on it. Sonya's face flushed as red as the petals of the flowers when I presented them to her.

"Thank you," she said as she accepted them and promptly held them to her nose. The tenderness in her voice and the way she cradled them told me she was a woman who didn't get flowers very often and appreciated the gesture deeply.

She put the vase on the table and sat down in the offered chair. One hand caressing the pink and red glass of the vase, she gave me a smile that made my chest tighten.

"They're beautiful, thank you." The tender tone of her voice told me how touched she was.

"So which do you like best? Yellow, white, pink, or red?"

The smile on her lush lips widened. "I love them all. It was so sweet of you to put one on my Jeep each day this week. You have the heart of a romantic." Gaze on the roses, she chewed at her bottom lip before answering. "If I had to choose, I would pick red. But why a dozen instead of one?"

I sat down across from her and gave her my most charming look. "Because tonight is our second date, and hopefully the start of something."

Her dark brows rose. "Something?"

"I don't want to define it yet and invite Loki to jinx it, but yeah, something."

Both brows rose at that. Candlelight danced across a nice flush in her cheeks. Before she had the chance to comment on my choice of words, the French patio doors opened. An older woman with long, silver hair draped over her shoulders, and a crisp white apron wrapped taut around her plump middle all but floated over to us. She held two glasses of water in her hands. Setting the water before us, she graced us with a warm smile, and removed a pencil and a notepad from her apron pocket.

"Aren't you two just the picture of adorable! I'm Gerty. I'll be your server tonight." Not giving us a chance to respond, she rattled off the menu of the night along with her wine recommendations.

She blushed at my smile as if she were half her age and indulged our every question with cheerful responses and fun banter. Sonya ordered tilapia with a pale ale while I chose prime rib with the house merlot. The waitress, who was also the B&B co-owner, jotted down our orders, beamed another smile at us, and returned to the house with an extra spring in her step.

Elbow on the table, Sonja's head settled into the palm of her hand as she watched our hostess all but skip away. "She's adorable." Her eyes narrowed when she turned them on me. "A red meat eater, huh?"

I grinned, knowing whatever her psychoanalyzing was coming up with, it was way off. "Yep, love it. That, and I saw her husband start prepping the dish early this morning, so I know he's been at it all day. I would feel bad if I didn't try it."

Sonya groaned. "Now I feel like a tool for ordering the fish."

I waved a hand. "Don't. He loves to cook, so you're doing him a favor."

"You sure?"

"Totally. You should see him at breakfast, whipping up everything under the sun when all I asked for was bacon." I laughed as I recalled him watching a cooking show while trying out a new dish. "It's a passion for him."

"Well, in that case, I'm glad I could contribute to someone's passion."

After a long drink of water, I relaxed back in my chair. "So, what are you passionate about?"

Her fingers splayed out to tap the side of her cheek as she thought about it. "Helping people, I guess. I want to help others move past loss, trauma, that kind of thing. I know a lot of people look down on psychologists, but that's why I changed my major." Her words struck a chord on many levels. That passion would make her perfect for her destiny.

"I think that sounds pretty noble."

A cute, snorty sort of laugh came from her. "Hardly. It comes from a place of my own pain, so in a way I'm doing it for myself. My dad was killed when I was a teenager, and I've spent a lot of time trying to deal with it. So, in a way, it's selfish."

"Now you're over analyzing yourself. You want to help others, that's rare in today's world, no matter what the reason."

Head tilting to the side, eyes widening a bit, she nodded. "True enough, I guess."

I leaned forward, wove my fingers together, and placed my hands on the table before us, close to her, but not quite touching. "That's horrible that you lost your dad so young, I'm sorry." I meant it, and I let it show in my eyes.

The look on her face softened, and she gave me a sad, half smile. "Thanks. He was pretty great, before…"

Clearly, she didn't want to finish the thought, and I wasn't going to make her. I knew where it was leading anyway, and I had no intention of pushing her to tell me that part. There was no reason; it would only cause her pain. Instead, I went a different direction. "What was he like?"

Her face lit up as she looked off into the shadows. "To everyone else— eccentric. To me, he was fun, attentive, and full of great stories." The sadness in her smile bit at me, but I could tell by her tone that she liked to talk about him.

"Stories?"

The candlelight revealed a flush in her cheeks, the second of the night. The color was so lovely on her, I resolved to put it back as often as possible, but in much better ways.

Her gaze moved to me. "Promise not to laugh?"

Straightening, I crossed my heart with a finger. "I promise."

Then she said the thing that opened the door wide. "My dad was an Odinist."

CHAPTER FIVE

SONYA

I watched him closely, waiting for the judgment that always came any time I revealed this to a guy I dated. They almost always ran or laughed. So many people misunderstood the religion of the old Gods and those who worshipped them. It was a big part of why I told guys I liked sooner rather than later. That way it hurt less when they turned tail or insulted my dad and made me turn tail. But with Raul being of Icelandic descent, I was hoping he might be different.

A puzzled look came over him. I braced myself as his mouth opened, closed, then opened again. "Why would I laugh? I'm an Odinist. My entire family are Odinist."

It was my turn to gape open-mouthed at him. After a moment, I said, "Well, that's a reaction I've never gotten." Then I began to worry. There were a lot of different types of Odinism out there. A few were even racist to a degree.

He held his hands up as if in surrender. "I know that look. Don't worry, not the false kind some use as an excuse for their fear and prejudice, but the kind that springs from the Gods themselves and the land blessed by them."

One eyebrow quirked up at his sincerity, I couldn't help it. He sounded so much like my dad had. When I didn't respond he went on. "You're not a believer."

I shrugged. "I'm not a non-believer." The puzzled look on his face as he half-cocked his head made me feel the need to explain. "Dad didn't push the religion on me, out of respect for my mom and her beliefs. She's full-blooded Cherokee. So, I ended up raised with two very different views on theology. It made me decide to be undecided, at least for now."

The warm smile that dimpled his cheeks heated me from all the way across the table. "I like that. So, what were your dad's favorite stories?"

Both his smile and the question turned my own lips up in response. "The ones about Fenrir, definitely." I had to look away into the flames of the fire pit to the left of us before I could go on. Dad's boyish grin was still fresh in my mind, along with the look of excitement and reverence in his pale blue eyes as he sat on the edge of my bed and told me the stories. No, not stories, he had said: tales from the Eddas, writings of things that had happened, or would happen, to the Gods.

Raul made a low humming noise of agreement. "Those are some of the best."

"Yes," I agreed. "My childhood was filled with tales of how the wolf Fenrir was so loved by the Gods that they took him from his father and raised him themselves. How they watched him grow, and grow, and grow, and became more and more wary of him as his strength increased. He was the son of Loki, after all, dad would say. Then about how their wariness led them to trick him into being chained. That part always made me sad."

The interest in his eyes warned me that I had said too much, that he would ask more pressing questions. I liked him. I didn't want him to know the whole truth just yet.

"Me too. But we believe the Gods are people, not like us exactly, but still people. And people do some foolish things when they're afraid. But even though they chained him, they loved him, cared for him, laughed, and played with him," Raul said. The way he said it, with such conviction and emotion, made it clear he believed in the stories as well. Interesting. Maybe he wouldn't freak like all the others did when they found out the whole truth.

"But he was still a captive."

"True. There's no way of excusing that," he acquiesced. "So, your dad liked the tales about the wolves the most?"

We were getting too close to the parts I didn't want to tell him. I hummed an affirmative noise, looking off into the dark again. "Not about just Fenrir, but Geri and Freki too."

"But did you like the tales as well?"

"I loved them," I admitted. "And I loved that my dad loved telling them to me. When I was really little he would tuck me in, and while he told me the story, we'd eat twinkies he snuck in without mom knowing." The memory made me smile and had my eyes misting up at the same time. As much as it hurt to relive it, it felt good too. And it helped steer the conversation another direction.

Raul reached across the table and covered one of my hands with his. "I'm sorry. I didn't mean to bring up something painful."

His thumb rubbed my hand in the most wonderful, distracting way. I looked up into his gentle golden brown eyes so filled with concern, and my heart thumped harder.

"You lost your dad, didn't you?" he asked gently.

"Yeah, a long time ago." When he went to prison, not when he died, but I wasn't about to say that.

His fingers wove through mine, distracting me again. The smile he gave me was kind of shy. "So, you don't have anything against us Odinists?"

The vulnerable look on his face was so cute that I smiled despite the pain still stabbing ghostly fingers into my chest. "Of course not. Prejudice is not my thing, in any form."

That cover model smile widened, then faded as his look turned pensive. "There are a lot of great tales in the Eddas. Why do you think your dad liked the ones about wolves the best?"

Oh damn. I shouldn't have said that. I shrugged. "Not sure." I was sure, and I couldn't let him catch on and press me about it. Telling him my dad believed in the Norse equivalent of skinwalkers wouldn't go over well. It never did. I turned his hand over and started tracing the lines of his palm. Bumps rose along his arm, and his eyes darkened with desire. "Enough about me. Tell me, what do you do for fun when you aren't traipsing around the forest."

"Well, I traipse around the forest a lot, both for work and for fun. I even love traveling to go traipse around other forests. I also enjoy kayaking, camping, football."

I groaned. "Oh no, not football!"

He made a pained sound and clutched his chest with his free hand. I laughed. "Please don't tell me you really don't like football! I was hoping you'd been joking before," he begged.

I shrugged. "I've watched too many guys come into the bar and use it as an excuse to drink their nights away and flirt with women who weren't their wives."

With a nod and a purse of his lips, he acquiesced. "I get that. But don't let those guys ruin it for you. It's an amazing game of strategy and teamwork."

"Well, when you say it like that, it doesn't sound so bad."

Long chestnut colored bangs fell across his golden eyes as he dipped his head to look coyly at me. It was both charming in a boyish way and dangerously sexy. "You're accepting and open-minded, a rare and beautiful thing." The way he looked at me when he said it made me think he wasn't just talking about my personality.

His thumb traced circles on the back of my hand, sending little sparks of heat through me. I dropped my head enough so the pieces of hair that had come free of my braid hid the blush heating my cheeks.

I shrugged. "I had a unique upbringing."

He laughed. "That's certainly something I can relate to."

A smile I couldn't fight turned up the corners of my lips. His easy laugh made dimples in his carefully crafted five-day scruff. Damn, the man was good looking. The shadows only served to make him appear mysterious and more alluring. My fingers wove through his and I found myself leaning over the table toward him. He leaned toward me, coming up off his chair. When our lips hovered less than an inch apart, the door to the B&B opened with a loud creak. We both lurched back into our seats like teenagers caught making out.

Grinning from ear to ear, our waitress floated to our table with a tray of drinks balanced on her left hand. The ease with which she twirled it, grabbing first one glass, then the second, and setting them before us, put several of my waitresses to shame.

"Here you go, darlings. Your meals will be out in a jiffy." With that, she spun on one conservative heel and started back for the door. As she turned, she caught my eye and winked.

Once the door shut behind her, Raul and I burst into laughter. After our laughter died down, he picked up his glass, took a long sniff, then a slow sip.

"Oh no, you're a wine snob," I teased in an overly dramatic tone.

His eyebrows shot up in a look of mock hurt. "Well, I wouldn't go so far as to say snob..." He let his voice trail off, then shrugged. "I just like to enjoy it with all my senses."

"Yep, wine snob."

"Hey!" He tossed his napkin at me.

I lifted my wineglass filled with beer, sniffed and swirled it, then took a long drink.

"Oh great, a beer snob," he said.

I threw his napkin back at him and erupted into laughter again.

We laughed, teased, and stayed away from hard subjects throughout dinner. Mostly we talked about different places we wanted to travel to. As before, his destinations all had to do with nature. Even though mine clashed with his, I told him straight up: Paris, Hong Kong, Tokyo, St. Petersburg, Karlstad, Sundsvall. He'd already been to more places than I thought I'd ever get to visit in my lifetime—especially considering my tuition debt. Six countries—if you counted Iceland and the eight times his parents had taken him as a kid, which I totally counted—on his list so far.

He invited me on a moonlit walk of the winery that I readily agreed to. Fresh, delicious night air, just warm enough to be comfortable without a jacket, blew across us and tugged at my hair. We walked hand in hand along a flagstone path leading through raised beds of flowers. The sweet scent of lilacs and gardenias almost made me sigh. This guy really knew how to take a girl on a date. But...

"You didn't need to pay for dinner," I told him.

"I'm all about women's independence, but I'm also all about being a gentleman. My parents raised me with old-fashioned values," he said.

"Old-fashioned?" My tone rose along with my inner hackles.

He held up his free hand. "Don't worry, not that old-fashioned. Tell you what, you can pay next time if it makes you feel better."

The tightness of his smile told me it would bug him to let me pay, but that he'd do it. Considering what I had left in my account would barely cover a loaf of bread and a jar of cheap peanut butter, I wasn't going to push the issue too much... this time. It struck me that I hoped there would be a next time.

Leaning against his shoulder as we walked into the rows of four-foot-tall grapevines, I tightened my grip on his hand. "Maybe next time I will," I said in a playful tone.

An easy silence fell for a while as we wove our way through the rows. The gentle breeze brought the sweet scent of ripening grapes and moist earth to my nose. Open as he seemed to be, this guy was an enigma. Leather-clad, dart catching bad boy and romantic gentleman weren't combinations I was used to seeing out here in "Hicksville," Idaho. Guys were generally one or the other. I felt like there had to be something about him I was missing. But that was probably my tendency to screw up a good thing rearing its ugly head.

"It's beautiful out here. Thanks for bringing me," I said.

The moonlight revealed his dimples as he grinned. "I'm glad you like it. I wasn't sure, after all your talk of visiting those cities."

I shrugged. "Admittedly, I'm both a city girl and a country girl."

"Well, it would be creepy if you were too perfect," he teased.

With a laugh, I bumped my hip into his. "What, like you?" My tone was only half teasing.

One side of his mouth quirked up into an amused look. He stopped walking, took both of my hands in his, and moved in front of me. Only inches remained between us. His woodsy, clean scent washed over me—not cologne, but honest-to-goodness outdoor guy scent. It tugged at something deep inside me. The way his golden eyes smoldered down at me ignited that something. His arms slid around my waist, pulling me against a chest that was as hard as I'd imagined it would be.

"I'm nowhere near perfect," he whispered as he bent toward me.

Not even my three-inch high, sexy, butt-kicking boots were tall enough to bring me to his level. But when I rose up on my toes, he bent at the knees and met me. The firm pressure of his lips against mine sent a bolt of heat shooting straight to my core. A growly, groan sort of noise that was altogether dangerous and hot rumbled from his mouth into mine. My body molded to his with a will of its own. Large biceps locked me in an embrace

I was in no hurry to leave. Gentle pressure from him urged my lips open. His tongue delved into my mouth. The wine and sweet sauce taste of him made me hungry for more.

Several long, thrilling moments later, he pulled back, leaving my lips throbbing and my breath coming in gasps. I wanted to grab him, throw him to the ground, and have at it right there. The thought of all the creepy crawlies and who knew what kind of bacteria stopped me. For once, I wished I was more of an outdoor girl, but maybe it was saving me from an impulsive mistake. Still, taking in his scruffy, runway model face coupled with all those muscles straining against his shirt kind of made me want to make all kinds of mistakes.

He brushed a finger across my lips, and I shivered. Chewing on his bottom lip, he pulled me in close again. "As much as I'd love to keep going with this, I don't want to rush things." The hard line of his erection disagreed. "You're too special."

"That's some line," I said, smiling to soften the sarcasm.

He shook his head and brushed my hair back from my face. "It isn't a line, I mean it."

Both his tone and expression told me he was serious as two fingers of Bruichladdich on the rocks. I pushed a hand playfully against his chest. "Great, now I've got to live up to that."

Laughing, he turned us around and started for the B&B, an arm around my waist. On the way back, I kept our conversation light and humorous even though I was feeling anything but. If he only knew how far I was from perfect, he might run for the hills he loved so much. Buried in student debt, I was unable to pay the light bill, let alone finish my psych degree. On good nights I went home smelling like liquor; on bad ones, liquor and vomit. I had dead daddy issues, and my mom was a pain pill addict constantly battling depression who I hadn't spoken to in years. I was about as far from special as a girl could get. And I was bound to disappoint him.

CHAPTER SIX

SONYA

A strong case of the feminine version of blue balls made for a restless night that had me sleeping late into the morning. I'd been sleeping so heavy, in fact, my phone nearly vibrated off the nightstand before I caught it. I bolted upright, my cheap cotton sheet pooling in my lap, and tried to sound like I'd been awake for hours.

"Hello?"

"Hey Sonja, it's Nikki."

Oh shit. How late is it? I held my phone away from my head for a second and checked the time. My shift didn't start for several more hours.

"What's up?"

"I know you're trying to get as many hours as you can, but can I talk you into letting me steal your shift tonight? Layla broke her wrist and I really need the extra cash," she pleaded, sounding all the more pathetic because I knew she was lying.

At least once a month she pulled something like this, coming up with a woe-is-me excuse for needing over time. She'd once claimed her dog had been hit by a car. She didn't own a dog, didn't even like animals. The woman had a horrible weakness for online shopping that bordered on obsessive. Today it worked in my favor, though.

"As long as boss man doesn't get pissed at me for letting you tend bar," I said through a sigh to make it sound good. Not that I thought she'd get suspicious if I gave in too easy, she was too dense for that, but I didn't want to take any chances.

"Don't worry, I already checked with him. Thanks so much, Sonja, you're the best!"

"Yeah, yeah, I know." I ended the call in the middle of her exuberant thank yous.

Tossing the phone aside, I sprung out of bed and headed for the shower. An hour later, I emerged blow-dried and knock out ready in a pair of skinny jeans black enough to match my hair and a silky gold top with a neckline deep enough to show off my girls. Digging in my knock-off Gucci purse, I found enough for a nice bottle of wine to thank Raul for the amazing date. Sure, it would mean PB&J sandwiches this week, but it was worth it. Part of me tried to feel all desperate and clingy for being the first one to reach out after our date, but I refused to fall into that ridiculous psyche trap. I liked him, he liked me; it didn't matter who reached out first or when. Glancing around my tiny Spartan-like apartment, I realized it was long past time for me to let someone else in—not just to it but also to my life. I'd been wrapped up into my medical studies for far too long. Nikki from work was the closest thing I had to a friend, and she'd never even been over. Hell, I didn't even have a fish, just a neat shelf of medical school books to keep me company. Med students didn't have time for things like a social life, and I was over it.

I stuck my favorite colored lip balm in my pocket and breezed out the door on a wave of caffeine and hormone-induced adrenalin. As much as I hated to admit it, this guy had awoken something in me, something that wanted to jump out and take hold of life instead of hiding in the bindings of a school book.

Humming to myself, I all but skipped to my Jeep parked in the complex parking lot. I jumped in, cranked the motor over with the screwdriver I kept in the center console and turned up Barns Courtney on the radio. Warm summer air poured in the windows. Today would be a hot one, I could tell already. But, at the moment it was tolerable and I didn't want to mess up my hair before seeing Raul, so I rolled up my driver's side window. With the hardtop off, it wouldn't do a ton of good, but it was better than nothing. I slipped my cheap convenience store sunglasses on and pulled out onto the road.

By the time I turned up the long gravel drive of the B&B, it was hot enough to make me glad there wasn't much to my silk top. I had to slow down to reduce the amount of dust the tires kicked up. The windows kept a lot of the wind out, but considering the top was off, they could only do so much. A few minutes later, I parked the Jeep next to Raul's Porsche in the small guest parking area of the B&B. Our two vehicles were the only ones here. Beside the German marvel of engineering, my half-restored Jeep looked so much like an ugly duckling that I cringed. Fun as the Porsche was to ride in, though, I wouldn't trade my Jeep for it. The car would high center on a curb, for the Gods' sakes.

Still, thinking of Raul behind the wheel, the long sleeves of his designer shirt rolled up over his muscular forearms as he wove us through the turns effortlessly, made me hot enough to wish I'd worn a tank top. I hopped out of the Jeep and started for the front door.

Sports car, designer clothes, and wine. This guy and I couldn't be more different, but I couldn't deny I was drawn to him.

As I opened the door to the B&B, I called out, "Hello?"

I entered a charming sitting room decorated in a country style with roosters and wine-related accents. The delicious aroma of something sweet and cinnamon-flavored wafted from the kitchen that lay through an arched opening off to the right.

"Come in, come in, dear," a woman's voice came from the kitchen.

I wandered in a few steps. Moments later, the co-owner and waitress from the other night emerged from the kitchen, wiping her hands on the checkered apron she wore. Flour dusted the disheveled grey bun atop her head and flecked her dimpled cheeks. The easy smile she wore told me that she was enjoying the hell out of herself despite being a bit of a disaster in the kitchen. I couldn't help but smile back.

"Oh, Sonya, welcome back, dear! You come to see Raul?" she asked.

I nodded, but before I could voice a response, she went on.

"Good, good! Sorry to say you just missed him, though. We've had several wolf sightings up in the hills, and he went to have himself a bit of a hike and a look."

"Oh. Well, I guess that's okay. I was hoping to buy him a bottle of your wine..." I let my voice trail off as I tried to revamp my plan.

"That is so sweet. Tell you what, let me grab that for you, and you can take it to him. He only left maybe fifteen minutes ago, and I bet you can catch up to him." The way she brightened, eyes widening and smile growing, made it impossible to say no. She turned and disappeared back into the kitchen while still talking, forcing me to follow her to avoid being rude.

"Nothing to worry about. The wolf isn't a danger to you. Mostly, they avoid people, so you likely won't even come across him," she said as she breezed around the kitchen.

"Oh, I know. Wolves don't worry me," I said only because it felt like she expected a response. Thanks to my dad and all his stories about wolves, I was almost as comfortable with them as I was with people. Much of my childhood had been spent visiting wolf preserves and hiking to find signs of them.

"That's good. I could tell you were a smart one right off the bat." She patted my cheek as she walked by.

She grabbed two cinnamon rolls from a cooling rack and wrapped them in parchment paper before putting them in a canvas shopping bag.

"White or red, dear?"

It took me a second to realize she meant wine. "Um...I honestly don't know which he prefers," I admitted.

"Red it is." She reached beneath the bar. After a bit of perusing, she added a bottle of wine and a corkscrew to the bag.

I dug in my jeans pocket for my cash when she tried to hand the bag to me. I had a sinking sensation my twenty wouldn't cover it. The woman waved her hand and shook her head.

"Now, I'll not be having any of that." She pushed the bag against my chest, forcing me to take it and abandon my search for cash. "Let an old woman feel like she's contributing to budding young love, please."

The smile she gave me, along with the pleading look on her face, made me sigh and nod. Emitting a little squeal, she clapped her hands together. Guilt nagged at me for not arguing more. I opened my mouth to do so. Chattering on about the location of the trail, she guided me to the patio door with a hand on my back, never giving me the chance to speak. We were out the door and stepping into the hot sun before I knew it.

"Think you can find that, dear?" she asked, finally giving me an opening.

"Yes, but—"

"Wonderful! You have fun now." With that, she spun on her heel and all but dashed back into the B&B.

Smiling, I shook my head at the French door as it closed behind her. I slung the bag over my shoulder, turned in the direction she had pointed me, and set out. Thanks to years of camping with my parents as a kid, and hiking and hunting with my dad, I had a great sense of direction. Whether or not "had" was the operative word remained to be seen. Confident and armed with sugary treats and wine, I set a fast pace through the grapevines. Bright sunlight beat down on my shoulders. I picked up my pace, both to make sure I got out of the sun as soon as possible, and to try to catch up to Raul. The hills, and the shade of trees with them, loomed not far in the distance. Maybe ten minutes away if I hurried.

As I walked, I kept an eye out for signs of Raul. There weren't many; a heel impression in the dirt here, a toe impression there. Soon the cool shade of the trees enveloped me. Fir trees rose up all around, reaching high into the powder blue sky, their feathery boughs extending out to intermingle. Ferns and other bushes competed for space around the base of the giants. Raul's prints disappeared. Thankfully, the pine needle-strewn path wound through the trunks in an obvious stretch of brown. If he hadn't followed it, I couldn't tell, and with all the underbrush it would have been obvious if he had gone another way.

The nice little trail quickly went from a leisurely forest walk to an uphill hike. I found my rhythm at a brisk pace. It wasn't exactly that I was in a hurry, only that this wasn't exactly my shot of whiskey anymore. Too many painful memories that had been good at the time came back when I was in the forest. Nowadays, my hikes were short, sweet, and usually outside of heavily forested areas. Everything sharpened; the pine and earth scents, the sounds of birds and squirrels, the fresh taste of the air, even the feel of the soft ground giving beneath my feet. And searching for something always gave me a rush. I'd forgotten about that. The last time I'd been hunting had been with my dad years ago. The thrill of finding the game had been the best part. He'd always said I was a natural at it, that it was in my blood, whatever that meant. Remembering all that hurt, a lot, which was exactly why I avoided forests.

The warmth trapped between my shirt and skin bordered on making me sweat. I hoped to catch up to Raul before my skin glistened. Sweaty funk wasn't the impression I wanted to make. At the risk of appearing a little slutty, I undid another button on my shirt so my girls could get some air. The instant relief of a cool breeze blowing down between my breasts drew a sigh from me. Refreshed, I leaned into the incline and attacked the hill with renewed vigor. My cheap knock-off hiking boots ate up the trail as I found my rhythm. As a kid I'd often shucked off my shoes and gone barefoot in the woods, loving the feel of the earth against my skin, but my feet weren't as tough as they used to be.

Birds sang out in protest as I surprised them by passing beneath their trees, but they couldn't be bothered to fly away. It made me confident that Raul had come this way because clearly the wildlife was already used to the presence of a person. I increased my pace. The incline grew steep enough that in places I had to grab at tree branches or secure rocks to steady myself as I climbed. After another twenty yards trees became scarce and boulders became frequent. The path all but disappeared. Ridgeline in sight, I kept going up, hoping I'd be able to locate the path again on top of it. Unfortunately, the sun beat down hot on me, unfiltered by anything this high up. But it only took a few more minutes to reach the top.

No plateau greeted me, only a rocky ridgeline a few feet wide and maybe a hundred feet long. Treetops stretched out across rolling hills in each direction as far as I could see. The path was gone. Letting out a long sigh, I tried to think like a wolf and imagine what direction I might go if I were one. Crazy as it sounded, I had a knack for finding creatures using that method. It was a big part of why Dad had loved taking me hunting. He'd always said I was a natural at getting inside heads.

I thought about why a wolf would come up to this ridge; to survey the area for game sights and scents, check scent markings left by other wolves or predators, check which direction water might be in. That last one struck a chord. Record high temperatures had been occurring all week. Water would likely be his highest priority. Why I thought of the wolf as a he, I wasn't sure. It just felt right.

Way down in a valley to my left, sunlight reflected off a thin winding sliver of silver.

"Bingo," I whispered.

It lay no more than two long hospital halls away. The way my mind automatically went to that comparison made me cringe. I'd had just about all the hospital halls I could handle in the one month I'd lasted as a volunteer. It had been what convinced me to switch to psych. Thankfully, I'd done it after only three years into my undergrad program. While I didn't love the idea of working indoors with only the scents of a leather couch and lavender diffuser to mask the sweat of nervous people, it was better than blood and death.

Picking the path of least resistance like an animal would, I started down the rocky hillside. The tree line quickly swallowed me up. Sweet pine scents filled my nose once the feathery boughs stretched overhead. A little thrill raced through me upon seeing the narrow animal path winding down through the underbrush. I still had it. I could almost feel Dad clapping me on the back and whooping with pride. Tears stung the corners of my eyes, but I blinked them back.

Now, hopefully, Raul followed the same path. The steep hillside forced my attention on my progress. In what seemed like no time at all, I reached semi-level ground and heard the trickling of water nearby. The air cooled to a tolerable warmth.

The sense that helped me find animals, told me they were near, prickled along my skin. There was no sign of Raul anywhere. At the water's edge, I crouched low behind a tree and waited. My gaze scanned the surrounding forest and the length of the small river. I didn't see anything. Experience told me to be patient and wait, so I did. From somewhere in the distance came a growl so full of menace that the hair on the back of my neck prickled and stood. Careful not to step on anything that would make noise, I sank back into the underbrush at the base of the tree. The sound had come from across the water. Still, something told me to stay out of sight. Dad had ingrained in me to always follow my instincts, so I did.

Across the water, ten feet or so up from the shoreline, I spotted the unmistakable shape of a wolf. The beast appeared to stand four feet at the shoulders. That was impossible. Thanks to childhood camping and hunting trips, and visits to several wolf preserves, I had seen my fair share of wolves. Never had I even heard of one getting that big. Maybe it was a trick of the angle, the light, or my perspective from my position. The unique blond, white, and gray coat was also something I had never seen. His beauty took my breath away. But he couldn't be a pure wolf and be that big, could he? Even if he were mixed with a dog, I didn't know of any dogs that got that big.

Prickles of something worked up my neck. It wasn't fear. This felt more like an awareness dredged up from deep inside, like part of me recognized the creature and felt a kinship. I'd always liked wolves, been drawn to them even. My Cherokee mom said they were my totem animal. But this was different. Maybe the clear mountain air was getting to me.

A low growl issued from the wolf, so quiet I barely heard it above the trickle of water over rocks. The curl of his lips from his teeth was unmistakable, though. I froze, not even daring to breathe. But he wasn't looking at me; he was looking further down the bank on his side of the river. A second wolf stalked out from behind a tree. Impossibly, this one was just as big. A black, brown, and white coat moved over muscles taut with tension. Menace radiated off the pair as they crept toward one another. Hackles rose in sharp lines down their backs. Teeth gnashed in warning as snarls were traded.

Mesmerized, I froze and watched. I wasn't sure which moved first; it happened so fast. The giants clashed with an eruption of menacing sounds. Teeth flashed, claws swiped, and fur flew. My eyes couldn't keep up. It was like watching a movie at twice normal speed. From this distance, I couldn't tell if blood flew as well, but it had to. Caught in the throes of their fight, they rolled behind a bush and out of my sight. One of the wolves—the blondish one—emerged from the other side, hackles raised and teeth bared, gaze riveted on the bush.

I waited, fearful for the other wolf. They were both such gigantic, rare beauties that I didn't want either of them hurt. But what stepped out of the bush wasn't a wolf, it was a man. Stark-ass naked as he was, I got a good look at every inch of his athletic body. Bright rivulets of blood stood out against his skin in multiple spots. Tattoos covered much of his arms and back, but from this distance I couldn't tell what they were. One set of gashes—from claws, I was sure—on his arm looked particularly bad.

When my gaze finally made it up to his face, I had to slap a hand over my mouth to suppress a gasp. It was hard to be sure from so far away, but I thought he looked a hell of a lot like Raul. The man maintained a fighting stance, hands out to his sides, fingers curled as if they possessed claws that could rake. Both he and the wolf snarled and growled at one another. That sound shouldn't have been able to come from a human's throat. It wasn't just a mimic of sound like most people could make; it was real. Hairs rose on the back of my neck. Any urge I had to step out and see if the man was all right, see if he might be Raul, fled. Something really, really wasn't right here.

They stood like that for a while, wolf and man glaring at one another. Challenge and menace weighed as heavy in the forest air as the sweet stench of liqueur did in a bar. The impossibility of the situation started to sink in, but I couldn't dispute what I was seeing. It occurred to me that I should say something to scare the wolf off. But I couldn't utter a sound. If this muscular man couldn't scare it off, how the hell was I supposed to? The man didn't act like he needed help. In fact, he didn't act like a man at all. That realization kept me frozen on the spot.

After several long, breathless minutes, they both eased out of their crouches, turned, and walked away from one another. I watched until both disappeared into the forest before I even dared breathe. Just to be sure, I watched another full minute. When I had counted in my head to sixty, I moved. Afraid of stepping on something and making noise, I walked sideways—one eye on the path, the other on the opposite bank. A little squeal almost escaped me when I smacked into what turned out to be a boulder.

Fear overcame reason. I turned and ran. Bushes scraped at me, tree branches smacked me, rocks turned underfoot, threatening to roll an ankle, but it barely slowed me. I didn't stop running until I reached the grapevines.

At the end of a row, I leaned on the vines' support structure until my chest stopped heaving in an attempt to get enough air. Somehow I had hung onto the bag with the wine and cinnamon rolls. Elbows on my knees, I breathed and tried to process what I had seen. The size of the wolves had to have been a trick of the light and distance. Maybe I had imagined the growl coming from the man. A stark-ass naked man in the middle of the woods who had appeared out of the very same bushes a wolf had just tumbled into. I couldn't explain that away.

But it wasn't Raul, it couldn't be. Right? I had to know for sure.

Straightening, I ran my fingers through my hair, smoothed my shirt, and pasted on a smile. I strode back toward the B&B on legs that still shook. If Raul was there, then he couldn't have been the naked man in the woods. Of course, that wouldn't explain why there had been a strange man in the woods naked and unarmed facing down a monstrous wolf. But at least it would mean it hadn't been Raul.

When I reached the back door to the B&B, I only paused for a second before going in. The sweat dampening my forehead could be explained by the heat. Now, if I could just stop shaking...

Still bent over the oven, Gerty called out a greeting. "Welcome back, dear! Will you be staying for lunch?"

I waved a hand, feigning a casual air. "Oh no, thank you. I was just dropping in to see if Raul is back."

Lips pursing, she shook her head. "Not yet. You didn't come across him, then. That's a shame." She nodded toward the bag I held. "Well, you're welcome to leave that in his room for him if you'd like."

I smiled and hoped I didn't look as disturbed as I felt. "That would be great, thanks."

"Right this way," she said, a delighted conspiratorial tone in her voice.

She led me down a hallway lined with doors and stopped before a dark blue one, opening it. Light filled the cozy room, pouring in through the massive three-pane sliding glass door that dominated the far wall. Wispy robin's egg blue curtains did little to obscure the view of a flower garden with grapevines stretching out behind them. Inside the room stood an antique-looking wooden desk, a four-poster queen bed, and a TV stand with a forty-inch or so TV on it. Paintings of grapes and winery related items added charm and splashes of color to the beige walls. Gerty dug a pencil and pad of paper from her apron, handed it to me with a conspiratorial smile, and left me to it.

The second the door closed behind her, I set to snooping. On the nightstand lay a book about the effects of the Arctic thaw on something called sunken forests. At first, I thought it might just be a book belonging to the B&B. But then I remembered Raul's love of all things forest-related.

That, and a bookmark poked out of the hardbound about two-thirds of the way through it. Not exactly my type of reading, but I could see Raul liking it. My mind conjured an image of him lying shirtless in bed reading. Though my body started to respond, the thought also made me think of the naked man in the woods facing down the wolf. Desire drained from me in a rush. I returned my focus to searching the room—for what, I wasn't sure.

No clothes lay on the floor, either in the bedroom or attached bath. Aside from him being exceedingly neat, nothing seemed out of the ordinary. Then I looked in the shower. The brand of shampoo and conditioner said *Lupine Naturals*. If I hadn't just seen what I had in the forest, it would have seemed like just a brand name. But... Prickles of ice danced along my skin. I backed out of the bathroom. My legs ran into something soft, and I jumped as a little yelp escaped me. I spun around, prepared to swing the heavy bag at someone, but it was only the edge of the bed. Fighting the impulse to run, I forced myself to set the bag on the bed next to the fluffed pillows. Because I knew Gerty expected it and might check, I wrote a quick note and dropped it next to the bag.

Sorry I missed you.

My mind was too frazzled to come up with anything else. It took every ounce of wispy control I had left to keep my pace at a walk as I left the room. Thankfully, Gerty was busy in the kitchen and let me get away with a simple goodbye. Once out of her sight, I speed-walked out of the B&B and to my Jeep. Only by a monumental effort did I manage not to throw gravel as I backed out, turned around, and started down the drive. The second my tires hit pavement, I shifted gears, hit the gas, and squealed around the corner.

As soon as a few miles lay between me and the B&B, I felt better. A few more and I began to feel silly. The whole thing seemed like a misunderstanding, a trick of light and distance made more sense than what my mind was trying to conjure. And I believed that until I was home alone and darkness fell outside. It reminded me of something I'd seen a long time ago. The similarities made the thought hard to banish. Every time I closed my eyes, all I saw were giant wolves and naked men covered in blood.

CHAPTER SEVEN

RAUL

After scrubbing the last of the blood from my body, I removed the showerhead and made sure I rinsed every bit of it down the drain. I'd managed to sneak in the sliding glass door to my room and avoid coming across anyone. But it wasn't just by luck. I had staked out the area from the cover of an oak in the garden before approaching. Explaining the gouges on my arm and blood wasn't something I wanted to do, especially considering I'd be healed by morning.

Damn Tyler Viðarrson. I hadn't realized this was his territory before I came here. That didn't mean I was going to back down, though. He lived in Montana, which meant, if he had claimed this territory, it was possibly because Sonya lived here and he knew about her. She was too important, and it was only a matter of time before everyone figured that out. She was already in enough danger with the few of us that knew now.

I was toweling off when my phone vibrated across the tile countertop. When I saw Morene's name, I snatched it up.

How goes the wild goose hunt?

I had to be careful how I answered, not because I didn't trust my sister, but because I knew how Bane monitored her phone. Just thinking his name made my fangs extend.

Not so wild. I found her, I texted back.

Thank goodness.

That struck a chord which resonated down into my body, sending unease shooting through me. I pressed her picture and clicked video chat. When she answered, all I could see was her chin and neck.

"Thank goodness? What does that mean? I detected a tone," I said.

My pulse sped. Why was she holding the phone down where I couldn't see her face? She laughed and I heard tension in the sound instead of humor.

"A tone? In a text, little bro? You're reaching," she teased. Her voice sounded strained and tired.

"In that case, why are you holding the phone where I can't see your face?"

Again she laughed, and the sound was thick, like maybe she'd been crying. "I'm not holding it. It's sitting on the counter, silly. I'm doing my hair. You did call out of the blue, you know."

"Because I'm worried about you."

"Well, you don't need to be. You found Bane's little "special lady". Now you can bring her to him, and we can get back to our plan of overthrowing him."

Nerves getting the better of me, I nearly poked myself in the eye with a brush. "Careful not to say that too loud." As his pack's proxy female alpha she was always surrounded by those loyal to Bane. "And there might be a slight problem with that."

"Problem? No, there can't be a problem. Do not let your romantic notions get in our way. Bane is getting suspicious of me. I need her here to distract him."

Dread prickled across me. "Suspicious? Are you in danger?"

"I can handle myself, for now."

"I'm coming back to petition the Council for permission right now. Please be careful around him."

"Always. But, little brother, hurry. And bring her with you."

The urgency in her voice had me running as I ended the call. I would petition the Council, and check on my sister, but there was no way I was taking Sonya into a literal den of wolves until she knew the truth.

Topping the Porsche out around 195 and meticulously checking my radar detector did me no good. When I reached Hemlock Hollow, Montana hours later the town hall was empty. A call to my father, alpha of the Reinhard pack, didn't gain me any ground either. My heart sank into my gut when he told me the next Alpha Council meeting lay two weeks away and my petition couldn't be heard until then. I couldn't explain why it was an emergency, not to him. He had no idea Morene and I were trying to infiltrate the Draupnir pack and take Bane down. As far as Father knew, Morene had stayed a member when Bane killed the prior alpha out of loyalty because it was her chosen pack. That was only partially true.

Left with no other option, I drove to Bane's house. The A-frame with a wrap-around porch emerged from the trees like a vulture with its wings spread, protecting its kill. Massive, triangular windows at the peak seemed to narrow at me like a raptor's gaze. I skidded to a stop, sending decorative gravel flying.

The front door opened and my sister came out, meeting me at the bottom of the steps before I could even set foot on them. Brown hair up in a messy bun, athletic frame wrapped in a knitted shawl, she looked a disheveled, frazzled mess. Clearly, she had not been doing her hair. As soon as she stepped out from beneath the porch's shadow, I saw it, the purple shade of a black eye. And it wasn't just her eye. The entire left side of her face appeared swollen.

A low growl tore from me. "Where is he?"

She stepped in my way and put a hand on my chest. "Don't overreact. It's from a challenger. They look much worse."

Gazing deep into her eyes, I searched for the truth. The slightest twitch of skin near her brow made me think she was lying.

"I am going to kill him," I growled as I pushed past her.

Fingers closed around my arm in an iron grip, reminding me she had earned her place as proxy female alpha. "I am not some damsel in distress who needs rescuing. Careful what you do next."

The unspoken words between her words cooled some of my anger. I couldn't afford to screw up our plans. I also couldn't walk away, not only as a brother, but also because Bane would get suspicious if I did. Taking a deep breath, I touched her hand and let her see the frustration in my eyes.

"Is it worth it?" I asked for at least the thousandth time since we'd developed this plan to take down the tyrant.

"Yes." After a dramatic breath, she went on. "Just do what he asks, and do it quickly."

I wasn't good with commands, and I'd had it with this bastard blackmailing me. Seeing my expression, my sister grabbed my shirt, yanked me to her, and whispered harshly in my ear. "We've come too far. Don't fuck this up."

I peeled her hand from my shirt. Brushing past her, I stormed up the stairs and threw the oversized front door open so hard it banged against the wall and rattled the front windows. Claws clicked on tile as three gray and white wolves rushed into the foyer. Jaws snapping, lips curling back, they did their best to intimidate me, but I stood my ground. I allowed my fangs to extend and gnashed them at the wolves.

"Get Bane now, or Odin help me, I will tear through each of you to get to him," I commanded.

Two of them wilted beneath the weight of power behind my words. The third flinched. They growled in answer, and each took a step closer to me. As *verndari*—protector—to the Draupnir alphas, they had no choice but to try and stop me. Not a single part of me felt bad for them. Their previous alpha—the one Bane had killed to take his spot—had been my mentor and good friend. These *varúlfur*—werewolves—had stayed after the battle and supported Bane. Every part of me itched to do what I threatened. I opened my hands as my fingernails grew into claws. Two of the wolves had the good sense to look worried.

"No need for such violence. Why is it always straight to violence with you, Raul?" Bane's gravelly voice preceded him, drifting in from the other room.

Lanky legs moving at a leisurely pace, the sinewy man all but slithered into the foyer. A black t-shirt clung to his runner's frame, tucked into camouflaged BDUs. The sides of his head had been freshly shaved to show off his Norse tattoos there, his long Mohawk of dark blond hair plated into a braid that went from his forehead to down between his shoulders. It stirred my anger even more that he affected the style of the Norsemen of old. He only pretended to honor the old ways, having used the ancient customs as a means to take his brother down and kill him legally.

"Because you bring it out in me," I said through my fangs.

With a wave of his hand, he told his *verndari* wolves to stand down. They relaxed their stances a bit, the hair on their backs smoothing. "Leave us," he told them.

Warning looks and growls cast my way as they did what their alpha bade them. Once the clicking of their claws faded into the house, Bane took a step closer, arms crossing over his chest. "You didn't bring her." The anger in his voice held an undertone of something I couldn't quite put my finger on—fear? Could it be fear of why I hadn't brought her?

"Of course not. I need to petition the Council for permission to bite her in."

Anger contorted his features, and he took another step closer. "No, you don't. You won't be the one to bite her in, therefore, that isn't your concern. Bring her to me and I will worry about that."

I cringed, not out of fear, but disgust. "You plan to turn her and make her your mate." The thought made me sick to my stomach. Sonya deserved better than that, better than him.

"What I plan isn't your concern either." He looked at the door before continuing. "But if you don't want to bring me Sonya, your sister is really proving herself as a viable candidate. I could make her the official female alpha rather than just proxy." The grin he gave me was all teeth.

Every muscle in my body wanted to shift and attack. I vibrated with the need. Forcing my instincts down, I spun away from him and stormed toward the door. "It won't come to that."

Laughter sounded on the other side of the door as I let it slam behind me. Morene flinched so hard the porch swing she sat in shuddered. No, I couldn't let it come to that. Becoming Bane's mate would kill my sister. And the determined look on her face told me she wouldn't hesitate to sacrifice herself for the cause. I had no choice but to bring Sonya to Bane.

CHAPTER EIGHT

SONYA

Aside from a text thanking me for the wine and cinnamon rolls and saying he couldn't wait to see me again, I didn't hear from Raul for two days. I started to question what I had seen. Then I rationalized it. Finally, I dismissed it altogether as an overactive imagination thanks to all the stories my dad had told me as a kid. It wasn't the first time my imagination had got the better of me.

In the middle of my shift on the third day, Raul texted me to ask if he could meet me after work. The sight of his name on my phone sent a thrill through me and made me smile. Despite the weirdness of the forest incident, I liked this guy, a lot. I wouldn't allow my weird upbringing to mess up whatever was building between us.

Love to. Off at nine, I texted back.

I couldn't stop smiling through the remainder of my shift. My tip jar was brimming. I searched the bar for Raul but didn't find him. Part of me was relieved I'd get to refresh my lipstick and check my hair, while another part worried just a little.

After a quick trip to the ladies' room, I stepped outside, re-rouged, with my hair free from its clips and brushed out. Warm evening air embraced me. The further into the parking lot I walked, the more I smelled pine trees instead of the bar's sickly sweet stench. I turned the corner to the employee parking lot. Through the trees I spotted Raul leaning against his Porsche, which was parked beside my Jeep. In blue jeans and his black motorcycle jacket, he looked a bit dangerous and sexy as all hell.

None of the trepidation I'd felt before returned. Being in his presence put me at ease, almost like something in him called to something in me. Whatever it was made me feel like I wasn't alone in the world.

Gaze roving slowly over me, he made a sound of appreciation that brought heat to my face. He pushed away from the car and produced a bouquet of yellow roses from behind his back. Accepting them with a smile, I buried my nose in them and inhaled.

"You shouldn't have," I said, totally charmed despite having told him I wasn't really a flowers kind of girl.

"Oh yes, I should have. I'm the one who's supposed to be giving you gifts, not the other way around. Thank you for the wine and cinnamon rolls, by the way."

I bristled a touch at the old-fashioned sexist notion. "It's the twenty-first century. A girl can get her guy gifts if she wants to."

Face lighting up so much those amber eyes of his glowed like they were trying to catch mosquitoes, he stepped close and slid an arm around me. "Your guy?" he asked as he nuzzled into my neck. "I like the sound of that."

The feathery sensation of his breath against my skin brought back the memory of our kiss. Heat spread throughout me. My breasts grew heavy in my bra, nipples hardening enough to threaten to give away my desire thanks to my thin, billowy blouse. I didn't care if he noticed. His hand slid slowly from my back and he opened the passenger door of the Porsche for me. Had it been an attempt to charm me because he wanted something, it wouldn't have worked. From our conversations, I knew he did it because he'd been raised to treat women with respect, which totally worked for me.

When he straightened back up, his arm wrapped tighter around my middle, pulling me against him. The scents of pine and earth wafting off him smelled so masculine and natural that a little sigh of pleasure slid from me. His chest rumbled his approval in a way that made my skin tighten deliciously. I met him as he bent down to kiss me. The soft touch of his lips made me hungry for more. My lips parted for him. Our tongues mingled, and he tasted so good it made me gasp. Deeper and deeper the kiss went, until our hands were exploring each other, and I was pressed hard up against the expensive sports car.

The last wisps of concern were torn away in the hurricane of desire that hit me. I wanted him right then and there.

Voices and the crunch of gravel warned us someone was coming and completely ruined the moment. He drew away and I got in the car before anyone could see me. My co-workers gossiped way too much, and it had to be one of them since we were in the employee parking lot. One of the waitresses came around the corner, the orange light of a cigarette illuminating her face. The Porsche roared to life and Raul pulled out of the parking spot. One hand on her hip, cigarette dangling from her lips, the waitress gave us a slack-jawed stare. I fought the urge not to hunker down in my seat. For one, the windows were tinted dark enough she shouldn't be able to see in. For two, I was a grown-ass woman who had every right to date who I wanted.

Raul laughed as we pulled out onto the road. "I take it she's going to give you grief over me," he said.

Groaning, I ran a hand through my hair. "Definitely."

When he turned his runway smile on me, my insides melted. "Then we'll just have to make it a night worth talking about."

While the food at dinner was amazing, the restaurant made me feel terribly underdressed. Most women wore nice dresses and heels that cost more than all of my college books put together, and most men wore suits. I was terrified of what the meal cost, especially after seeing the menu had no prices. That was never a good sign.

Raul put me at ease by joking quietly about the stuffy patrons and assuring me he expected nothing more than for me to have a good time and enjoy good food. None of my tail was expected in exchange for the lobster tail, he had teased. He insisted that he'd been looking for a good excuse to eat at the place and just hadn't wanted to go alone. The man's charm and laid-back manner put me at ease. And it turned out he could be quite funny.

Though we had traveled nearly an hour to reach what passed for a city in these parts and would have a long drive home, I agreed eagerly when he suggested we go for a walk in a local park. I didn't want the night to end. It had been years since I'd had so much fun with a guy.

We pulled into the parking lot and before I could reach for the handle, he had popped out and shot around to open the door for me. Like a gentleman of old, he took my hand and helped me out of the car.

The heat of his hand in mine shot straight to my navel. The moonlight made his strangely beautiful eyes appear to glow. Before I could focus on them too much, they closed and he bent to kiss me. His firm, but soft, lips distracted me from my misgivings yet again. Our tongues explored each other's mouths as our hands explored each other's bodies. His physique was hard in a way one could only get from a combination of working out and using their muscles. It made me think he did a lot of hiking as a forest ranger. Before that train of thought could lead me down a disturbing path, his hand palmed my right breast, and my thoughts scattered.

I ground my hips against his. The hardness that awaited made me want to strip him down then and there and have my way with him. It was dark and secluded enough that we just might get away with it. The thought sent a thrill through me. I reached for his belt.

Laughter blew to us on a breeze, and young voices followed.

Our kiss ended abruptly and we parted. Taking my hand back up, Raul meandered toward the path. I gave him a coy smile as I licked the taste of him from my lips.

"Guess we got carried away," I said in a breathless voice.

He made a humming noise in his throat that made muscles between my legs tighten. "You have that effect on me," he said.

My smile grew. I like that I affected him. "Let's go to my place," I said without thinking. This wasn't something I wanted to overthink. Right now I wanted him, and that was all that mattered.

One brow raised, his tongue darted out to touch his top lip. "Are you sure?"

I let my gaze rove slowly over him. "Oh hell yes."

Wiggling my eyebrows at him, I pulled him into a faster pace alongside me. We resumed our play of chasing, catching, and kissing one another on our way back through the park. Exhilaration fueled my steps. Not only had it been a long time since I'd had a man between my legs, but Raul also made me feel wild and carefree—like I had been before med school. It made me realize how badly I wanted to be that person again; free of doubt, stress, and debt. And the hot man teasing and laughing with me made all that real and possible again. We were almost back to the car when he grabbed me around the waist, literally swept me off my feet, then froze, body rigid—and not in a sexy, jump your bones kind of way.

I looked into his eyes only to find him staring off into the darkness. A prickling at the back of my neck made me run a hand over it. The feeling only intensified. Breath held, I followed Raul's fierce gaze into the darkness. Light reflected off two almond-shaped eyes the color of ice. I'd never seen blue wolf eyes, but I knew beyond a doubt that's what they were. The shadows hid all but those eyes and hints of fur. Yet something deep inside told me it was a wolf. And those eyes were so far off the ground it had to be the biggest wolf on the planet.

I let go of Raul, squirmed my way free of him, and started to back away. The car sat only a few steps behind me. Raul put himself between the wolf and me. It would have seemed valiant—if not outdated—if his crouched posture hadn't reminded me so much of the guy in the woods with the wolf. A low growl full of menace and warning sounded. It wasn't coming from the shadows. It came from Raul. But that was impossible. It wasn't a sound a human throat could make, nowhere close.

My foot slid off the curb and a squeal of surprise erupted from me as I fell backward. Raul's Porsche broke my fall after only a few inches. I spun around and scrambled for the door. After what felt like an eternity, my fingers found the handle and I tore it open. A flash of guilt made me pause and look back to check on Raul. It appeared he had advanced toward the wolf a few steps.

"Come on, Raul, before you get bit!" I called to him.

He started to walk backward toward me. Once he reached the front end of the car, I got in and slammed my door shut. In a literal heartbeat—so fast I didn't even see him move—Raul was suddenly climbing in the driver's side. The Porsche roared to life and we tore out of the parking lot fast enough to throw me back in my seat.

Raul let out a whoop followed by a nervous laugh. "That was crazy, right?" he said through a smile that looked forced.

I didn't smile back because I was afraid it would turn into a terrified grimace. "Yeah. What the hell is a wolf doing in the middle of town?" I asked. And why was it so freakishly huge? I wasn't about to voice that question and sound completely crazy.

Glancing in the rearview mirror, Raul answered, "I'm pretty sure it was a cross with a Newfoundland or something. Probably someone's dog."

My brows rose in disbelief. "You really think so?" I couldn't keep the disbelief out of my voice.

He waved a hand dismissively as he took a forty-five mile per hour corner at sixty-five. "Definitely."

I supposed he could be right, but still... "That was very valiant, in an old school knight in shining armor kind of way, but you didn't have to throw yourself in harm's way for me," I said.

Giving me sort of a crooked, half-smile, he put his hand on my knee. "Sorry about that. I didn't mean to get all alpha male on you. Don't get me wrong, I'm all for a powerful woman who can take care of herself. Instinct just kicked in."

Warmth spread through me, promising to banish the weirdness of the night if I let it. I covered his hand with my own, not sure if I wanted to remove it, or slide it higher onto my thigh.

"Instinct?" I asked.

The wistful look he gave me made the warmth spread—until I saw him check the rearview mirror again. Why would he keep doing that? A wolf-dog wouldn't exactly follow us onto the highway.

"Maybe not instinct so much as teaching. My parents raised me with old-fashioned values mixed with modern views. It stuck."

"Hmmm. I think I'd like your parents."

The laugh that escaped him had a harsh edge. "Maybe. They can be... strict. But they'd like you, I'm sure of it."

That stunned me to silence. Fear of the "meet the parents" conversation made me desperate to distract him. I moved his hand higher up my leg. "Well, I like *you*."

Eyes widening a bit, he gave me a panty-dropping smile that made me want to do just that. "I like you too, a lot."

Despite the fireworks of nerves those words set off in me, I smiled. I wanted to give this a chance. My hang-ups from my odd upbringing would not ruin this for me. It had just been a dog, after all. It was totally coincidental and separate from the incident in the woods—an incident that had nothing to do with Raul. And the fact that he kept looking in the rearview mirror and accelerating was also totally coincidental. Totally.

CHAPTER NINE

SONYA

Caught up in the moment as I was, I didn't see fate coming for me. I should have. There were signs, like the animalistic growl rumbling in his chest as he kissed a wet line down my jaw to my neck. I wasn't about to protest. The primal sound of it was sexy as hell, even if it did remind me of all the strange things I'd seen over the last week. His incredible amber eyes developed a shine about them that seemed unnatural, but I figured that was the drinks we'd had earlier getting to me. It had to be that, along with my wild imagination. His hips ground against mine, pushing me into the door to my downstairs apartment.

Again he asked to go inside, and again I refused. I certainly had nothing against premarital sex, but casual sex was another thing altogether. Especially with a guy I had only met two weeks ago. What had I been thinking when I'd invited him back here? It was bad enough that we were making out in the dark alley in front of my low-income apartment where my sketchy neighbors could come out at any moment. But then, Twin Falls, Idaho, wasn't exactly a hopping town after midnight. And seeing as my apartment building was only a little two-story number that housed less than fifty, the odds of anyone being around were slim to none. All the more reason not to go inside where temptation would lead me somewhere I wasn't willing to go yet.

Not anymore. I needed to process the weirdness of our date and make sense of it first. Something strange was going on here; I felt it deep in my bones.

The gentle nips at my neck grew harder. Walking that razor edge between pleasure and pain made my blood pump so hard the cool Idaho night felt more like Arizona in the midst of summer. Until impossibly sharp teeth grazed the sensitive skin of my neck.

"Ouch!"

Those teeth broke through my skin and sank deep into the muscles and meat of my neck. I screamed and writhed in pain but he had locked onto me with the strength of a boa constrictor. After an excruciating few seconds, his teeth withdrew from me in a rush.

One moment he was pressed against me, the next he leaped back and stood against the building across the alley as if using it to brace himself. His mouth hung open and within it, not one set of fangs shone in the streetlight, but two; a set on the top and a set on the bottom, much like a canine. The worst part; they were covered in my blood. My *blood*.

"What the hell?" I yelled, a hand going to my neck.

My fingers came away slick and sticky with blood. He stood there, staring at me with those gleaming eyes, blood trickling over his bottom lip. Slowly, like a cat's claws, his fangs retracted until they looked like no more than overly pointy teeth. Before tonight I had thought his toothy smile looked sexy. Now, not so much. If it weren't for the blood making a steady trail down his chin, I would have thought I'd imagined the whole thing. Then there was the pain.

Keeping my eyes on him, I fumbled in my pocket for my keys while the other searched for the mace I kept on me. My fingers settled around the metal canister. Hand so steady it surprised even me, I took it out, flicked my thumb under the safety cap, and pointed it at him. The bastard just grinned, though it was a sad smile instead of one filled with humor. A cold chill of fear threatened to extinguish my anger.

"What. The. Hell?" I demanded slower, emphasizing each word, desperate to hang on to the anger that gave me courage.

His shoulders sagged, his defined chest caving in on itself as if he were trying to melt back into the wall. The button-up shirt he wore lay splayed open, giving me a good view of the blood that dripped from his chin onto his pale pecs. Only moments ago I had opened that shirt in my eagerness to touch his bare flesh. The memory made me shiver with revulsion. That gorgeous, fit body of his suddenly seemed to sport more hair than I remembered. Hair covered his bare chest where I didn't recall him having any before, and the line of it from his belly button down into the waistband of his jeans had definitely thickened. My hand holding the mace began to shake, and I loathed myself a little for the weakness. He looked past the mace at me with something close to contempt.

"I'm sorry it happened this way. I didn't want it to, I swear." He glanced down the alley, then back at me. "Sonya, please, come with me and I'll explain everything."

Straightening, he adjusted the erection pushing against the fly of his jeans, as if I weren't pointing mace at his half-naked body. The front step swam a bit. Damn, how deep had he bitten into me? I pressed one hand to the wound and kept the mace trained on him with the other. Freaked out and feeling exposed, I wanted nothing more than to dig my keys out of my jeans pocket and open my apartment door, but I didn't dare. Dropping my guard even a little wasn't an option.

Hot, sticky blood oozed through my fingers and ran down my neck. "You *bit* me, you son of a bitch!"

"I'm sorry. I ran out of time." Going stiff, he stood up straighter, eyes darting down the alley in both directions. The alley swam, and not in a pleasant, too-much-Jack-Daniels kind of way.

"Get away from me, Raul. Now," I said, doing my best to sound like the badass I totally did not feel like at the moment.

"No, Sonya. Listen, I'll explain everything, but you need to come with me now," he urged, reaching a hand toward me.

Soft yellow light from headlights outlined his spiky brown hair. Someone had parked at the other end, beyond the small bit of green space that edged the building. When the lights didn't switch off, I realized whoever it was wanted to see us. I called out for help. The blinding bright light hid Raul's expression from me until he turned his back to it. Damned if he didn't look a bit toothier—and worried. The second part I liked; the first made me even more concerned than I already was.

He backed away and started down the sidewalk, moving away from the headlights. "Damn him. I will come back for you and explain everything," he said in that sexy voice of his that made me want to vomit.

***

Thank you for reading! Did you enjoy? Please Add Your Review! Every review helps authors and encourages readers to take a chance on a book.

And don't miss more in the Children of Fenrir series with book one, BITTEN & BEHOLDEN, a full-length novel. Turn the page for a sneak peek!

You can also sign up for the City Owl Press newsletter to receive notice of all book releases!

SNEAK PEEK OF BITTEN & BEHOLDEN

Caught up in the moment as I was, I didn't see fate coming for me. I should have. There were signs. Like the animalistic growl rumbling in his chest as he kissed a wet line down my jaw to my neck. I wasn't about to protest. The primal sound of it was sexy as hell, even if it did remind me of all the strange things I'd seen over the last week. His incredible amber eyes developed a shine about them that seemed unnatural, but I figured that was the drinks we'd had earlier getting to me. It had to be that, along with my wild imagination. His hips ground against mine, pushing me into the door to my downstairs apartment.

Again he asked to go inside, and again I refused. I certainly had nothing against premarital sex, but casual sex was another thing altogether. Especially with a guy I had only met two weeks ago. What had I been thinking when I'd invited him back here? It was bad enough that we were making out in the dark alley in front of my low-income apartment where my sketchy neighbors could come out at any moment. But then, Twin Falls, Idaho wasn't exactly a hopping town after midnight. And seeing as my apartment building was only a little two-story number that housed less than fifty, the odds of anyone being around were slim to none. All the more reason not to go inside where temptation would lead me somewhere I wasn't willing to go yet.

Not anymore. I needed to process the weirdness of our date and make sense of it first. Something strange was going on here, I felt it deep in my bones.

The gentle nips at my neck grew harder. Walking that razor edge of pleasure/pain made my blood pump so hard the cool Idaho night felt more like Arizona in the midst of summer. Until impossibly sharp teeth grazed the sensitive skin of my neck.

"Ouch!"

Those teeth broke through my skin and sank deep into the muscles and meat of my neck. I screamed and writhed in pain but he had locked onto me with the strength of a boa constrictor. After an excruciating few seconds, his teeth withdrew from me in a rush.

One moment he was pressed against me, the next he leaped back and stood against the building across the alley as if using it to brace himself. His mouth hung open and within it, not one set of fangs shone in the streetlight, but two. A set on the top and a set on the bottom, much like a canine. The worst part; they were covered in my blood. My *blood*.

"What the hell?" I yelled, a hand going to my neck.

My fingers came away slick and sticky with blood. He stood there, staring at me with those gleaming eyes, blood trickling over his bottom lip. Slowly, like a cat's claws, his fangs retracted until they looked like no more than overly pointy teeth. Before tonight I had thought his toothy smile looked sexy. Now, not so much. If it weren't for the blood making a steady trail down his chin, I would have thought I'd imagined the whole thing. Then there was the pain.

Keeping my eyes on him, I fumbled in my pocket for my keys while the other searched for the mace I kept on me. My fingers settled around the metal canister. Hand so steady it surprised even me, I took it out, flicked my thumb under the safety cap, and pointed it at him. The bastard just grinned, though it was a sad smile instead of one filled with humor. A cold chill of fear threatened to extinguish my anger.

"What. The. Hell?" I demanded slower, emphasizing each word, desperate to hang on to the anger that gave me courage.

His shoulders sagged, his defined chest caving in on itself as if he were trying to melt back into the wall. The button-up shirt he wore lay splayed open, giving me a good view of the blood that dripped from his chin onto his pale pecs. Only moments ago I had opened that shirt in my eagerness to touch his bare flesh. The memory made me shiver with revulsion. That gorgeous, fit body of his suddenly seemed to sport more hair than I remembered. Hair covered his bare chest where I didn't recall him having any before, and the line of it from his belly button down into the waistband of his jeans had definitely thickened. The hand holding the mace began to shake, and I loathed myself a little for the weakness. He looked past the mace at me with something close to contempt.

"I'm sorry it happened this way. I didn't want it to, I swear." He glanced down the alley, then back at me. "Sonya, please, come with me and I'll explain everything."

Straightening, he adjusted the erection pushing against the fly of his jeans, as if I weren't pointing mace at his half-naked body. The front step swam a bit. Damn, how deep had he bitten into me? I pressed one hand to the wound and kept the mace trained on him with the other. Freaked out and feeling exposed, I wanted nothing more than to dig my keys out of my jeans pocket and open my apartment door, but I didn't dare. Dropping my guard even a little wasn't an option.

Hot, sticky blood oozed through my fingers and ran down my neck. "You *bit* me, you son of a bitch!"

"I'm sorry. I ran out of time." Going stiff, he stood up straighter, eyes darting down the alley in both directions. The alley swam, and not in a pleasant, too-much-Jack-Daniels kind of way.

"Get away from me, Raul. Now," I said, doing my best to sound like the badass I totally did not feel like at the moment.

"No, Sonya. Listen, I'll explain everything, but you need to come with me now," he urged, reaching a hand toward me.

Soft yellow light from headlights outlined his spiky brown hair. Someone had parked at the other end, beyond the small bit of green space that edged the building. When the lights didn't switch off, I realized whoever it was wanted to see us. I called out for help. The blinding bright light hid Raul's expression from me until he turned his back to it. Damned if he didn't look a bit toothier—and worried. The second part I liked; the first made me even more concerned than I already was.

He backed away and started down the sidewalk, moving away from the headlights. "Damn him. I will come back for you and explain everything," he said in that sexy voice of his that made me want to vomit.

Light bounced off the green thread of the top rocker sewn to his black jacket. No matter how many times I had asked, he'd never told me what AVW—stitched onto the top rocker—stood for. The bottom rocker read Montana, revealing he belonged to some kind of group out of that state. Beyond that, I knew very little. Between the rockers sat a patch with strange symbols of circling knotwork woven into the shape of a canine with Norse runes all around it. That told me even less. Damn it, I should have known better.

"Not a chance, you freak. You ever come back here and I will kill you."

I couldn't even bring myself to kill spiders, but he didn't know that.

White teeth flashed in a snarl that was directed at something behind me before he dashed off. I wanted to follow him, make sure he left, but I couldn't move. Hell, I couldn't hold the mace up anymore. Before it could fall, I shoved it in my pocket, having to try twice. Soft footsteps padded from the direction of the headlights. While my fuzzy mind regretted having pocketing the mace, part of me realized it was probably a concerned neighbor who had heard me yell. But none of my neighbors were as tall and muscular as the man who came running down the alley toward me. I wasn't sure if it was the light, or if he had short golden hair, but one thing I couldn't miss were his ice-blue eyes. A woman could get caught in eyes like that. The man looked like he'd walked right out of one of the old Norse legends my dad had liked to tell me when I was a kid.

Everything swayed. Or maybe it was me; I couldn't tell. Strong hands gripped my arms, holding me upright. The skin of his hands tingled against my arms, growing warmer the longer he held on, until it felt like we might melt together into one. Something in my fuzzy brain tried to tell me that wouldn't be a bad thing, not at all. Those ice-blue eyes snagged my gaze and held on with a vengeance. Heat to rival that of an inferno lay behind those glacial blues and it pulled at me as if it wanted to consume me.

"You should get inside and lock the door behind you. I will go after him." His voice was accented with the right timbre to set my nerves vibrating in a very good way.

Survival instincts broke through the haze caused by blood loss. Yeah, that had to be it, the blood loss. I thrust my hand in my pocket and pulled out my keys. As I turned them in the lock, I forced my weary head up so I could look at the blond man one more time. I wanted to remember his face, and not just because he was the only witness to the assault on me.

"Careful, he's dangerous," I warned.

"So am I. Do not worry about me. I will be back to make sure you are all right," he said.

I turned the knob and nearly fell as the door opened inward. Just before I closed it, I heard the man curse in a language I didn't recognize but that tickled at my memory. Several sets of footsteps pounded on the pavement. I slammed the door shut, threw the deadbolt, and bolted the other two locks for good measure. On weak legs I made my way to the bedroom, using the walls and furniture to keep myself upright. Coagulating blood forced me to peel my hand from my neck so I could use it.

Blood ran in a hot trail from the wound, down my neck and between my breasts. In this light I couldn't tell by the color alone how bad it was, but the flow was entirely too steady for my comfort. The fact that my heart was working overtime from the stress surely didn't help. Halfway there, with my stomach threatening to revolt and my vision swimming, I realized I should have grabbed my cell phone off the coffee table. Too late now. Besides, I didn't want the cops involved. Damn police only made things worse, a lesson I had learned all too well growing up. I'd go back for the phone in a moment and call Nikki from work. She'd take me to the hospital faster than an ambulance could get here. First, I had to stop the bleeding, and I was closer to the bathroom than the living room. Shock would soon slow my heart and with it my blood flow, giving me plenty of time to get to an ER. With six years into my medical degree I could do just as much—or more, in most cases—to stop the bleeding as an EMT anyway.

Hoping I didn't split my head open on the doorframe, I let go of the wall and took a leap of faith by crossing the open space to the bathroom. My hand left a bloody streak on the door as I stumbled through. The vanity offered me something stable to lean on and was thankfully at the right height so I didn't have to lift my hand to do so, because at that point, I didn't think I could.

From within the vanity mirror my ghost stared back at me. Or at least that's what it looked like. My bronze skin looked sickly pale, a hue I strove hard to avoid with as many hours in the sun as I could manage while working full time at the bar and studying for med school. Blood stained my straight-as-an-arrow black hair, making it cling to my neck and left breast. I didn't want to peel away the hair, didn't want to see, but I had to. Swallowing my fear, I pulled my hair away. The pain caused my vision to go dark, but it came back after a few blinks.

Bright red blood flowed from not one but four sets of holes, two above and two below my carotid. They weren't deep enough to show muscle or bone, but the sight of them was enough to make my stomach twist. I definitely should have grabbed my cell phone. I could have at least called one of the waitresses from the bar to come get me. With one hand bracing myself against the sink, I opened the vanity with the other and grabbed the hydrogen peroxide. The way I figured it, a biker guy with a bizarre biting fetish and weird teeth was likely to carry some kind of germs. Even if he didn't, I wanted to boil the freak's saliva from my skin and this was the best way I could do it without actually using boiling water.

White-hot agony exploded into my neck as I poured the bottle of peroxide onto the wounds. My vision went black and this time it didn't clear.

Don't stop now. Keep reading with your copy of BITTEN & BEHOLD.

And find more from Heather McCorkle at
www.heathermccorkle.com

Read book one, BITTEN & BEHOLDEN, a full-length novel, available now, and find more from Heather McCorkle at www.heathermccorkle.com

As the chaos of Loki covers the earth again, will the Seeker awaken to save us all?

When Sonja Michaelson's hot date turns into something from a horror movie, she wakes up with a chunk taken out of her neck, and her body going through strange changes. Her attacker has disappeared, leaving her a mysterious note to meet him in Montana.

With her senses tipping over into the freaky, she is left with no choice but to go after him.

Instead of her attacker, she finds Tyler Viðarrson, an alluring man who claims he's been sent to teach her how to survive the transition into her new life. Ty informs her that she's been bitten into a line of werewolves that trace their lineage back to an ancient pack of Icelandic Vikings.

Now, several packs are fighting for her to join them.

If she doesn't learn to control her wolf by the full moon, she could lose what's left of her sanity. But with such a tempting teacher, she fears her sanity may be the least of her worries.

Sonja soon discovers there is a larger and more sinister plan at work. She is not the only one who has been changed against her will, and whoever is changing the others, wants her for what she can awaken – an ancient power that may endanger the entire world.

Please sign up for the City Owl Press newsletter for chances to win special subscriber-only contests and giveaways as well as receiving information on upcoming releases and special excerpts.

All reviews are **welcome** and **appreciated**. Please consider leaving one on your favorite social media and book buying sites.

For books in the world of romance and speculative fiction that embody Innovation, Creativity, and Affordability, check out City Owl Press at www. cityowlpress.com.

ACKNOWLEDGMENTS

First, thank you for reading. Each and every one of you inspire me daily to keep at this crazy life of writing. Without you, we authors would have no purpose. Secondly, I owe this novel largely to my critique partners who insisted I tell Raul's side of the story, and wouldn't let me rest until I got it right. Also, I have to thank Yelena Casale, my amazing editor for being so enthusiastic about bringing this story to light and deepening the world of the Children of Fenrir series.

ABOUT THE AUTHOR

HEATHER McCORKLE is an Amazon bestselling author of paranormal romance, historical romances, urban fantasy, and steampunk. She lives in the Great Northwest with her amazing husband and horizontally challenged cat. As a Native Oregonian, she enjoys the outdoors as much as the worlds she creates on the pages. When she isn't writing, reading, or editing, you can find her on the ski slopes, or prepping for ski  season by hiking, mountain biking, and paddleboarding. She has been known to play an excessive amount of disc golf, but still claims to be mediocre at it.

www.heathermccorkle.com

twitter.com/HeatherMcCorkle
instagram.com/heathermccorkle
facebook.com/authorHeatherMcCorkle
pinterest.com/heathermccorkle

ABOUT THE PUBLISHER

City Owl Press is a cutting edge indie publishing company, bringing the world of romance and speculative fiction to discerning readers.

Escape Your World. Get Lost in Ours!

www.cityowlpress.com

f facebook.com/YourCityOwlPress
🐦 twitter.com/cityowlpress
📷 instagram.com/cityowlbooks
📌 pinterest.com/cityowlpress

www.ingramcontent.com/pod-product-compliance
Lightning Source LLC
Chambersburg PA
CBHW051248180626
46816CB00004BA/1386